I0602500

THE STUDENT

SKYE WARREN

CHAPTER ONE

Firehose of Knowledge

A DRIZZLE ENVELOPS Tanglewood University. A thunderstorm would be better. Or clear skies. Instead, this in-between draws a haze through the air. It's as if the clouds are doing that slow, silent cry where tears leak out, drops quivering on eyelashes before falling.

"Thanks," I say, breathless, as I lug my duffel bag down the tall steps of the bus.

The driver grunts in response.

I step onto the curb and turn around—just in time to be splashed by the heavy tires going through the water-logged street. Rainwater drips down my chin. It soaks my long-sleeved T-shirt, leaving the fabric tight against my breasts.

Wet denim hugs my thighs.

At least my body managed to block my duffel bag and all the books inside from most of the spray. Hooray?

The bright side is looking more dim these days. It would be easy to sit down on the slick pavement and let the earth reclaim me if I didn't have a mission.

I start the walk towards my dorm.

It's not that long. I make this trek every day from the campus bus stop to Hathaway Dormitory, but it feels like a million miles when I'm weighed down with an entire puddle. All I have to do is drop off my stuff, and then I can go to campus security.

A chill seeps into my bones.

If they won't help me, I'll go to Dean Morris. Whatever works.

The campus stretches out like a living tapestry, each thread a building steeped in history. Ivy clings to the brick walls of stately structures, their gargoyles watching like sentinels. Massive oak trees provide shelter from the rain, their leaves whispering secrets only they understand.

The heavy academic aura suffocates and dazzles at once. It should feel like home, but it doesn't. I belong here on paper, but in my heart, I'm still that broken girl from Port Lavaca, wondering how I slipped through the cracks into this rarefied world. It always feels like someone is going to realize an error has been made, that I'll be summarily removed from campus.

Not smart enough. Not rich enough. Not even pretty enough.

Overall, not enough.

The library looms ahead, its gothic architecture intimidating under gray skies. But for me? It's just a fortress where I never quite fit in.

I pass by Whitney Hall—the building where Professor Stratford taught last semester. My heart does that annoying flip when I think of him. His voice echoes in my mind, confident and smooth like dark chocolate melting on my tongue. But I swallow hard. This year is about moving forward.

Hathaway stands a little apart from the other, fancier buildings as if they don't want to get too close. The air in the foyer hits me like an icy blast.

A group of guys pass by, shouting and shoving each other in that playful, competitive way that college boys do.

"Nice nips," a guy says, and they all laugh.

I look down to see that, yep, my nipples are hard and visible through the pale pink cotton. Embarrassment heats my cheeks, bringing a stinging warmth to frozen skin.

The old elevator carries the dampness with me to the fourth floor.

Outside my room, I pause.

There's most likely someone inside. A stranger. Someone to replace Daisy, even though that's impossible. We've been together since freshman year. Is she okay? The question has haunted me the entire winter break.

The lock yields to my old key.

The door swings open.

Shock holds me in its frigid grasp.

I'm standing there, dripping onto the thin carpet, mouth open, tears welling in my eyes. Because Daisy reclines on her bed, leaning against propped-up pillows while she pages through some kind of engineering text that probably weighs as much as she does.

"Daisy." My voice comes out as a croak.

"Hey," she says, flashing me a bright, quick smile. "You're back. Come inside and change your clothes before you catch your death."

She sounds breezy and casual and…ordinary.

"Daisy Mae Bradshaw."

"Wow, what's with the 'middle name' calling? I'm happy to see you too. How was your Christmas? Did someone knit you a sweater? Et cetera, et cetera."

"Et freaking cetera? You disappeared."

She rolls her eyes.

She. Rolls. Her. Eyes. That's it. I'm going to

kill her.

"I left you a note."

"Yeah, a note that said you were going home. Where you *belong*. Which is obviously code for being kidnapped and forced to write the note at gunpoint, because you don't belong there. You belong here."

"I went home, just like you went home. I'm sorry we couldn't sublet an apartment together the way we planned, but I needed some time away from Tanglewood. Now, are you going to dry off or are you going to get pneumonia?"

Frustration is probably enough to warm me, but I come inside anyway and close the door. I have to peel the clothes off me. Even my bra and panties are damp. I don't bother with new ones, pulling a fresh T-shirt and jeans on over clammy skin.

Then I join Daisy on her bed and drag the textbook away from her. I shove her thin notebook inside to keep her place because I'm not a monster.

"I called the school administration, the sheriff's office, and the FBI. They're very interested in your little not-a-cult commune, by the way. But no one could help me get in touch with you."

She blinks. "Um. Why?"

"Because I thought you might be hurt. Or dead. Or *married*, for God's sake."

"I specifically said in my note *not* to worry."

I spent hours on the phone, dialing different people. I even charted an elaborate bus route that would take 46 hours to complete, though what I would do when faced with electric fences I didn't know. Worry had waged a war inside me even as I put on a placid face to shlepp pancakes and watered-down coffee around a diner. How could I not worry?

I'd rather be angry at her. I'd prefer the heat of indignation to the cold, gnawing fear that clawed at me for weeks.

Instead, my lower lip quivers.

Now that I have a chance to pause and catch my breath, now that the tepid warmth of the dorm has started to thaw me out, I can see the brittleness of her smile, the chaotic lights in her blue eyes. The very rigid way she holds herself in an intentionally casual position, as if trying to convince me—or perhaps herself—that everything is fine.

She's not nearly as blasé as she appears. Underneath that careful façade, I can sense the tremors of something deeper, something she's trying desperately to hide. Pain. Yes, I recognize pain, even if there are no visible bruises.

My throat tightens. "Can I hug you?"

She swallows hard, her eyes flickering with a mix of emotions that she's trying so hard to keep at bay. "You're making a big deal out of nothing. I'm fine. You're fine. Everyone is fine. But I'm not into hugging. Okay? Not right now."

Not right now.

Which probably means she has bruises. Places I would hurt if I squeezed her like I want to, just to reassure myself that she's really here and not some sort of rain-inspired fever dream. She's not really fine. I'm not, either. But we're back at Tanglewood University, and maybe for right now, that's good enough.

"I was going to go to campus security. Then the administration. I was going to march right into Dean Morris's office and demand they do something."

"You know they would say it's none of their business what happens off campus." Daisy's voice is resigned, her blue eyes avoiding mine.

"It's their business if you had just been traumatized while *on* campus. They can't just brush it off." I feel a surge of protectiveness, my hands clenching at my sides. "I won't let them."

"It was just a prank. Nothing serious."

Her attempt at nonchalance doesn't fool me.

I would not call leaving someone freezing cold and half-conscious in a fountain in the dead of night to be a prank. It's criminal, but I'm not going to argue with her about that.

Not now, when she's so fragile.

"If they didn't listen, I had a backup plan. I was going to take it to the Tanglewood Tea. They have a voice, and I'd make sure they used it."

Daisy shakes her head, her blonde hair catching the light. "As if they would care. It's not exactly the hottest gossip like they usually post."

"I would make them care. They have a valuable platform, and we'd need it."

Her laugh is unsteady, a mix of gratitude and disbelief. "Thank you for caring enough for that. Really."

"We still can take it to them," I say, nudging my knee against hers, the barest hint of human contact, maybe the most either of us could take. I have a feeling that after a summer spent at home, I have a wild light in my eyes, too. "Someone should pay for what they did."

"Let your handsome professor worry about it."

"He's not my professor anymore," I say, too fast, before realizing that my voice is shrill. It's important that I won't have any classes with him. I checked my spring schedule three times to make sure. "I mean, he was never mine. And he's not going to take them down."

"He's not?"

"He's part of the Shakespeare Society. One of them, back when he was a student here. And now he's back to lead them. Or protect them. I don't know."

Blonde eyebrows rise. "Sounds like I missed a lot."

I force a shrug. "Not really. It was a boring break. I worked at the diner."

"Then you probably have enough money for textbooks." Her voice is definitely casual, but I can read the question in them. Or actually, the accusation.

"No."

"No?" she asks, drawing the word out. "They don't tip well at the trucker stop?"

"They don't, but that's not why I don't have money."

She sighs, resigned. "You gave it to them."

"They're my parents."

"They *lied* to you. And stole from you, basically."

"They can't steal what I gave them. And I

don't know about the lie."

"You said they admitted it."

"Yeah, but…"

It's hard to explain the strange vortex in which my parents live. Even after confronting them, even after hearing them admit the cancer was never real, they still maintain the pretense. The pretense that she has chemotherapy. That she might not get better.

It's the fabric of their lives, as real as the beams holding up the ramshackle house.

I'm not sure they would know who to be without it.

"I started reading up on Munchausen syndrome. It's a real disorder that—"

"Oh God. You're using your love of research to excuse her."

"She's actually losing weight. Her hair is falling out."

"How?"

"I couldn't figure it out. People with Munchausen have been known to inject themselves with medicines or even toxins to produce the symptoms they need. I looked through her stuff, but I couldn't figure out what was doing it."

"So you gave them all your hard-earned diner money."

I rub my eyes, exhausted. "I know I'm an idiot."

Her hand takes mine, her fingers cool but soothing. Her gentle squeeze compels me to meet her blue gaze. "You're not an idiot. You're a kind person. A wonderful daughter. Better than they deserve, but then the world is hardly ever fair."

"It's different when I'm there. Like we have to believe in these things with blind faith, and any questioning is a betrayal. I know we give you a hard time, but maybe my family is the cult."

"All families are cults."

"That sounds…a little extreme?"

"Think about it. Children need their parents for survival. Which means that parents can do anything, and the kids have to not only take it, they have to love them. That's all love is, in the end. A survival mechanism."

I crack a smile. "Now you're going to study anthropology?"

"I already know how people work. That's why I'm in engineering."

"Well, I envy you, then, because I don't understand people at all. That's why I'm in literature. Poetry, plays, novels. They're sips of knowledge."

"You want to know people? Sex is a firehose of

knowledge."

I groan. "The visuals, Daisy. The *visuals*."

A light laugh. "I'm going to the hotel tonight. Are you coming with me?"

"Shit."

"Of course you're coming with me. The only question is how long it's going to take me to style your hair so you don't look like a bedraggled street urchin about to clean a chimney."

Sex. With a stranger.

Can I do it?

If I want textbooks this semester, I don't have a choice.

They've taken most of them online, which they say is to help us avoid breaking our backs by carrying them around. I'm not sure if that's the real reason or if it's so they can kill the used textbook marketplace. Now we have to pay the same full price we would have paid for a shiny new thick textbook for digital access.

Which means I'm screwed.

Literally.

That's okay, though. Maybe having sex will wipe away the memory of Professor William Stratford's hands on my breasts, his cock in my mouth, the memory of his hard masculine grunt as he climaxed, his body holding mine as if in a sheltering embrace.

It was a lie, just like my mother's cancer.

Maybe Daisy has the right idea.

Love is nothing more than a survival mechanism, a story that I tell myself in order to endure what I need to endure, a fiction that makes it more palatable. As Hamlet said, *there is nothing either good or bad, but thinking makes it so.*

CHAPTER TWO

Money is no Problem

I THOUGHT I built the Pinnacle Hotel up in my head. It couldn't possibly have been that grand. No. Somehow, it's even more luxurious. Gorgeous opulence and old-world charm combine with just a hint of modernity in its sleek screens.

This is the kind of place I would dream about coming to.

That is, if I were coming for any other reason than finding a man to sleep with, so I can pay for my textbooks.

Again.

Except this time there won't be any lying, betraying backstabbing professor to take my virginity and give me the most incredible orgasm of my life. No, this time, there's going to be some random old guy, and you know what?

"This is for the best," I say, hoping I sound confident.

Daisy surveys the small crowd of elegantly dressed people. "What is?"

"This whole prostitution thing."

A woman with white hair in abundant curls piled on her head looks askance as she walks by. Oops. I probably shouldn't have used that word out loud. Daisy snort-laughs.

"I mean, it's for the best that I have sex with someone else."

Daisy glances back. "And why's that?"

"So that I can move on." It's time that I learned how to get on in this world and stop believing in fairy tales. Like the fact that a handsome older wealthy man like Professor William Stratford might be interested in little Anne Hill.

"Ah." Daisy gives me an enigmatic Mona Lisa smile.

"You don't believe me."

"What I believe doesn't matter."

"Fine. I'll prove it to you."

I hop onto one of the brass-and-velvet stools as a bartender approaches. "Give me one shot of whatever you have that will get me drunk. Gin, rum, spades—"

"That's a card game, not a liquor." Daisy sits beside me.

"Whatever. I just need it to be cheap."

"Coming right up," the bartender says.

"Are you sure about this?" Daisy asks. "You haven't drunk enough to have tolerance for liquor."

"Of course I am. I'm serious about doing it, which means I need something to help me through. Ideally, I won't even remember this."

The shot arrives, clear liquid that could honestly be water in a little crystal glass. I hold my breath the way Professor Stratford taught me to. I still remember his velvet voice telling me it's the air that makes it burn.

I put the glass to my lips and tip my head back. It slides down my throat without a burn. Nice. I hold my breath for one more second.

And then finally take in a gulp of air.

There's a slight burn, but not nearly as much as there would be if I'd breathed normally. Though… Wow, that aftertaste. It's not good. It's kind of like I mixed the cleaner I used to clean my parents' house with the bayou where the industrial compound dumps its waste.

"Another," I say, flagging down the bartender. "Give me another one." Another clear liquid shot arrives. How easy.

I drink it carefully, cringing at the taste.

"This is gonna end horribly," Daisy says.

"Another round," I say, but the bartender is busy on the other side. "Another drink. Seriously, where is this guy? I need another drink. *I would give all of my fame for a pot of ale and safety!*"

Daisy snorts. "You don't have any fame."

"Well, I don't need that much ale."

"If you're quoting Shakespeare, you're already drunk enough."

"I can quote Shakespeare when I'm very, very sober."

The bartender finally returns.

"Another," I say.

"Water," Daisy says. "She'll have water."

The bartender unfortunately listens to her, not me.

"Daisy. I need to take this seriously."

"I believe you, but clients don't tip nearly as well if you vomit on them."

"Holy shit. This is the *best* water I've ever had."

"Oh my God. We're so screwed."

We're approached by a man in a rumpled business suit. I give him a vague smile, sure that he's here for Daisy, who, as usual, looks like a bombshell. Daisy has to nudge me hard, her elbow in my ribs, before I realize he's speaking directly to me.

"You from around here?" he asks.

"Not really," I say, drawing out the words, trying to think of a lie that sounds cute and flirty and not like I'm awkward as hell. "I'm just here for the night."

"Me, too." A smile softens his severe face.

It's a handsome face.

If I were a 60-year-old woman, that is.

The wrinkles are a lot to take in. I don't think that I'm ageist or anything, but it's different when I'm thinking of going to bed with a stranger. His hair is completely gray, a little silver on the sides. That could make him look dashing, but the stain on his tie ruins the effect.

I tell myself it doesn't matter.

"So what do you do?" This is definitely not the conversation Daisy would make, but she's not helping me at all. And this guy, for some reason isn't on her side of the bar.

No, he's over by me, leaning close, looking down my dress.

This isn't one that I borrowed from Daisy, which means that it actually covers up the girls. The deep V-neck still gives him enough to appreciate. At least that's what I'm assuming, by the way he's been staring at my rack since he got here.

I picked out this little number at Goodwill when I was buying jeans to replace the ones stained with coffee from the diner. The dress was a splurge. A completely unnecessary purchase. It has a spare, elegant top part made of blue silk and a thigh-hugging asymmetrical bottom with large ruffles.

I won't admit to anyone, least of all myself, that I imagined myself wearing this on a date with someone like Professor Stratford. No, not someone *like* him. Exactly him. The version of him that I believed I knew. Before the night I found out everything was a lie.

Now I'm wearing the dress to have sex with someone.

That should properly destroy any latent fantasies.

"Oh, business analysis and consulting," he says, which tells me nothing. That's the point, I presume, but it also doesn't leave me much to make conversation with. "Crunching numbers."

I force myself to smile. "You must be tired after all that work."

That seems to be all the invitation he needs, and he leans in close.

Close enough that I can smell the sour whiskey on his breath.

"Not too tired to get to know you. You look absolutely ravishing, my dear. A truly beautiful young woman."

I feel my cheeks heat. Why do the words seem so freaking inappropriate coming out of his lips? His wrinkled, eighty-year-old lips? Actually, I have no idea how old he is. I am not good at guessing people's ages, but I can't hold back a small, visceral shudder.

"Thank you?" I manage to squeak out. I go for a sip of water to clear my throat.

"You remind me of my granddaughter."

That sip of water sprays all over him as I try not to choke to death at the shock of hearing those words. "Excuse me," I say, gasping. "Something got caught in my throat."

I take the napkin Daisy thrusts at me, my hands trembling as I dab at the man's shirt, now speckled with my misdirected sip of water. "I am so sorry," I murmur, heat rising to my cheeks, not just from embarrassment but from the sheer discomfort of the situation.

To my surprise, he doesn't react with irritation or dismissal. Instead, there's a flicker of amusement in his eyes, as if he finds me endearing. Maybe it's because his granddaughter shares these same awkward traits. The thought churns my stomach, a queasy reminder of the bizarre compliment he paid me moments ago.

"Don't worry about it," he assures me, his voice a soothing balm that does nothing to ease the unease twisting inside me. There's a warmth to it, a gentleness that's almost paternal—grandfatherly, even. Yet, his smile now carries an edge that feels unsettling, like a shadow passing over a sunlit room. I never knew my grandparents, but part of me wishes they could have been as kind and understanding as he appears to be.

I'm gonna throw up.

"It was a surprise," he continues, seemingly oblivious to my inner turmoil. "What I said. I understand that. It's…" He hesitates, as if sifting through a mental thesaurus for the most precise term. "A little taboo."

A little taboo. His words echo in my mind, a gross understatement that barely scratches the surface of this interaction. A little taboo is the sort of thing you whisper about in hushed tones, like a forbidden romance with someone off-limits, like your supervisor at the coffee shop. That's *a little taboo.* But this? This is a plunge into uncharted waters, murky and deep with undercurrents I'm not sure I want to understand.

"Yeah," I force out, my voice barely above a whisper. "That's what I meant. Taboo." I offer him a weak smile, hoping it will suffice as a period at the end of this uncomfortable sentence. But as his gaze lingers on me, I can't shake the feeling that this conversation is far from over.

"Taboo can be fun. You don't mind, do you?"

The question hangs in the air like a challenge, and I feel my heart pounding in my chest, a frantic rhythm that matches the chaotic whirl of the hotel bar around us. I send Daisy a glance over my shoulder that I'm sure is wild-eyed. We didn't come up with an emergency messaging protocol, but I'm pretty sure she'll understand this one. It means, please make this stop. But Daisy's face is a mask of calm, her blue eyes unreadable as she sips her drink, her attention seemingly focused on the jazz band playing in the corner.

He takes my hands in his, and oh God, his fingers, they're so cold. Is he dying? Is he already dead? It's possible I shouldn't have had that second shot. The alcohol was meant to be a social lubricant, not a gateway to my own personal hell. "I would love to go upstairs with you," he says, his voice a low rumble that sends shivers down my spine. "I'm going to call you Jasmine. And you're gonna call me Grandpa."

Oh my God. My mind races, trying to find a way out of this, but my throat constricts, rendering me mute. This isn't what I signed up for. This isn't the kind of taboo I've whispered about in hushed tones with Daisy during late-night study sessions.

"Of course," Daisy says from behind, giving my hip a little squeeze that he can't see. Even without an established emergency messaging protocol, I can tell it means, *suck it up because you came here to do a job.* "It will cost extra."

"The money is no problem," he assures us, a sly grin spreading across his weathered face.

Oh great. The money is no problem. Meanwhile, I have to learn to say, *Yes, Grandpa, give it to me harder*, in the time it's going to take the elevator to bring us up to a room that feels as confining as a prison cell.

I take a deep breath, trying to steady my racing heart. The thought of escaping into the pages of a Shakespeare play is tempting, but I'm here, trapped in a reality that's slipping further away from the academic dreams that brought me to Tanglewood University. Kill me now, I think, but then I remember why I'm here.

The textbooks, the tuition, the chance to break free from the oppressive chains of my past—it's all riding on this moment. I have to be strong, for Daisy, for myself.

I have to survive this night.

I vaguely sense that Daisy is negotiating some insanely high price for the privilege of having sex with someone who looks like his relative. I can't really understand what they're even saying, because my ears are ringing.

"Let's go," he says, tugging me gently from the stool.

Unfortunately, I'm short, which means I can't glide gently from this height. Instead, I tumble awkwardly, trying to keep my legs together so I don't flash the entire bar. I land splattered against him. And I can feel that he's already hard through his slacks.

Oh God.

"Oh no, did you hurt yourself? We'll go to my room. I'll take care of you."

"I don't think so," comes another voice, this one lower and somehow more powerful even without a body to match it to.

CHAPTER THREE

One Little Kiss

GRANDPA TURNS, HIS mouth dropping open.

His surprise is nothing compared to mine.

Professor William Stratford stands there looking dashing as hell.

I blink, trying to shake off the haze of surprise.

Professor Stratford stands at the entrance to the bar, radiating power, his suit molded to a lean muscled frame. He looks like a battle-hardened knight, ready to charge in and slay the grasping dragon.

Except, of course, he is the dragon.

I hate the traitorous flash of relief I feel of gratitude that he came for me. Even though that doesn't make any sense. He didn't come for me. He must just, I don't know, live at this hotel or something. That's why he managed to be here the two nights I've ever been here. Nothing else makes sense. I don't believe in coincidences.

Oh, and I forgot, I hate him.

"Excuse me," I tell him. "We have somewhere to be." And with that, I take Grandpa's withering hand and lead him towards the bank of elevators.

Professor Stratford barks a small, incredulous laugh. "I don't think so."

He puts a hand on Grandpa's shoulder and squeezes. Grandpa is not a particularly small man, but he winces. Professor Stratford must be squeezing hard because his knees almost buckle. "Don't you have an important phone call to take?"

"Yes," he mutters, not quite meeting my eyes. "Maybe some other time, Jasmine. Don't tell your mother."

And then he's gone, leaving the faint scent of talc powder in his wake.

Professor Stratford raises a dark eyebrow. "Jasmine?"

"Don't ask," I say with a scowl.

"Oh, I'm definitely going to ask. I have a lot of questions."

How dare he?

Righteous anger fills my veins, which is nice because now I'm out whatever ridiculous amount of money Daisy negotiated for me. How dare he come here and interfere?

Sure, I did not actually want to go upstairs with that guy, but that's not the point.

How dare Professor Stratford show up and look so frustratingly handsome in his suit, so strong and muscled and vibrant? Professor Stratford isn't nearly as old as that man, but he's definitely older than me. His age doesn't diminish him. It makes him more powerful.

And I hate that about him.

"What the hell are you doing here?" he says, his voice low.

"What am I doing here? What are *you* doing here?"

"Not soliciting, that's for damn sure."

"Are you here for another gala or charity ball or whatever other events rich people invent to show off their clothes and talk about how many yachts they own?"

Those coffee-colored eyes see right to the heart of me. And they are disturbingly kind behind the frustration on the surface. "No, I'm not here for a gala. I'm here to keep you from going upstairs with some random man who is probably diseased and possibly violent."

"Like you?"

"Yes," he snaps. "Like me, like anyone who you don't know. Anything could happen to you up there. You can't be this trusting, Anne."

"That's Ms. Hill to you," I say, jabbing him in his stupid silk tie on his stupid flat abs. That feel hard as steel even beneath the pointy tip of my finger. "Now I need to find another grandpa."

"What the hell are you talking about?"

"She might be a little drunk," Daisy says from behind me.

"Christ."

"I'm only drunk," I explain, "because I want to have sex with a random old guy."

"You're not having sex with anyone."

"This is outrageous. I'm outraged. I needed that money. How else—"

"How do I expect you to buy your text-books?" he asks, because he's a know-it-all. Professors are always know-it-alls. I think it's a job requirement. "They're being delivered to your dorm room right now. Yours, too, Ms. Brad-shaw."

"Well, unlike her, I'm not outraged," Daisy says. "Thank you very much, Professor Stratford. Though if you're bringing her back to campus, I'll stay here, if you don't mind."

"I do mind," he says. "We're leaving."

"We are *not* leaving," I say, though I'm not entirely sure what I'm fighting for right now. It's something to do with strength and independence and the fact that he smells so good. It's all a little bit fuzzy in my brain right now.

My voice has risen because people are looking over.

"Fine," he says. "Let's have a conversation about it. Privately."

Only somewhat chastened, I allow him to lead me, his hand on the small of my back, into a dark hallway. Somehow we end up in a supply closet full of boxes.

I read some of the labels out loud. "O'Connell Monument Whiskey. IBEX Premium Vodka. Handmade in small batches. Louis XIII Cognac RARE CASK Collection. This is a lot of alcohol. Like how drunk could I get if I drank all of this?"

"If you get any more drunk, you're going to fall over."

"I'm not even that drunk. I'm just tipsy."

"Tipsy enough to go upstairs with a creep."

"That's the whole point of this field trip. Going upstairs with a creep. And I don't know why you're so mad about it. I did it with you."

"That's right. It's hypocritical and commandeering and I don't give a shit."

"Though you weren't really that creepy."

A reluctant puff of laughter escapes him. "Not *that* creepy?"

"Not creepy at all," I tell him, though there was some reason I was supposed to stay angry at him. I shouldn't tell him that he made me feel so good that I can't sleep because I want him. That every other boy around me looks like just that—a boy. He's a man.

And then he kisses me, leaning me back against the door, tipping my chin up with his thumb. It's a short kiss. When he pulls away, I find myself leaning forward to prolong it, my lips seeking his warmth, his tenderness. The kiss might be a lie, but it's a sweet one.

Then he's standing at full height, shaking his head at me, disapproving.

I can't even believe it. Disapproving, as if he isn't the one who kissed me? As if he isn't the one who's part of some crazy secret society that's endangering people?

"Here's what's going to happen. I'm going to put you and Daisy in a cab. You're going to take an Advil and drink a full glass of water and go to bed early, because you have school bright and early tomorrow morning."

Part of me recognizes that he's right.

That is probably what's going to happen.

The *other* part of me, the part that enjoyed the kiss, the part that's furious and attracted at the same time, wants to make him suffer a little bit.

And I'll make him suffer by kissing me.

It makes complete sense in my head.

"We don't have to leave right away," I say, leaning back against the door.

His gaze flashes down to the deep V of my dress, and it feels like a victory. He scowls. "Actually, you do."

"Not really. We have enough time for you to call me Jasmine and make me call you a—"

"Don't say it. I'm not old enough for that."

I grin. "But you are old."

He curses under his breath.

"I don't mind, honestly. That's not why I hate you. I hate you because—"

"I know why you hate me."

"It should make me not attracted to you. Like people I hate shouldn't be handsome, sexy professors who understand Shakespeare references."

He puts his hand on the bridge of his nose. "This must be penance. I would ask God what I've done to deserve this, but frankly, there are too many options."

"It's because you're not a nice person," I explain to him.

"Exactly, which is why we need to get you home."

I don't have a home. The dorm doesn't count. "Just one little kiss."

"We already kissed."

"That one was short. One little, longer kiss."

His gaze goes to my lips.

My eyelids drift shut. "I want to remember what it felt like that night, the night you met me here. I was so nervous. So afraid. And then you took me upstairs and made me feel good."

When I open my eyes, he's only an inch away, those golden flecks standing out in the dark of the storage room. Somehow his hand's behind my neck, tilting me up to face him. His other hand is on my hip.

"Goddamn." His voice rubs together like gravel.

"You made me feel so good," I say again, plaintive. "Can you do it again?"

I'm not even sure what I'm asking for, a hotel room? No, that's not what I want. At least I shouldn't want that. And it's not what he gives me. Instead, there's a burning kiss, his hand covering my breast, his thumb brushing against my nipple.

"God, your body should be illegal."

I giggle. And I never giggle, but somehow the alcohol has done this to me.

Or maybe it's just him. He's like some kind of liquor, a drug. Something that makes me act in ways that I normally wouldn't.

He kisses me again. And then I'm lost in the moment and the pleasure and the feeling of his hand sliding up my thigh and then between my legs where he cups my pussy with possessive command, with the firm press of ownership.

Professor Stratford's hand tightens on my hip, his breath hot on my ear. "You think this is a game?"

I can't answer, not with his fingers tracing the lace of my panties, not with his thumb circling my clit. My breath hitches, and I arch into his touch. The space is dark, but his eyes glint in the sliver of light from the entrance. He's angry at me. It only makes his touch feel like fire.

His hand slides under the fabric, and I gasp as he strokes me, slow and deliberate. "You were going to let some stranger touch you like this?"

I shake my head, but my hips move against his hand, betraying me. He finds a rhythm that has me clutching his shoulders, my breath coming in quick gasps. Pleasure builds, and I'm close, so close—

His movements slow to agonizing languidness.

My climax drops out of reach.

His fingers move again, slower this time, building me up with agonizing precision. I moan, my nails digging into his shoulders. He brings me to the edge again, and again, he stops.

I whimper, trying to move against him, but he holds me firm. That's when I realize he's doing this on purpose. A frustrated sound escapes me.

A dark chuckle. "Do you need something, Anne?"

He's playing my body like an instrument. "Please."

His fingers circle my clit, and I'm so close, so close—

He stops again, and I cry out in frustration. His lips curve into a smirk. He's not going to let me come. Not until he's ready. Not until he decides.

"Why are you doing this to me?"

He leans in, his lips brushing mine. "Be a good girl for me."

His fingers move again, and I'm lost, lost in the pleasure, lost in him. I'm begging, pleading, and he's commanding my body. In this dark shadow, in this secret moment, I'm completely at his mercy.

Desire has made me delirious. "What do I have to do?"

"If you want something from me, you may beg."

He pinches my clit, hard enough that my lips open on a harsh gasp. No words come to me like this. I'm desperate and hungry. Some distant part of me recognizes that I should refuse his demands. Begging will change the balance between us. It will weaken me. Then he presses gentle, whiskery kisses against my throat, and I lose any will to fight this, to fight him.

He prompts me, his voice. "*Please, Professor Stratford. Put your fingers inside me. I need to be filled by you.*"

Oh God. "Please, Professor Stratford. Put your fingers inside me. I—"

The words dissolve as he presses one fingertip into my core, circling such a sensitive place, dragging the wetness around. "Am I making this hard for you, dear heart? Good. I like to see you struggle."

"I need to be filled by you," I say, the words coming out in a rush.

My body responds before my mind can fully process his question, two of his fingers pressing into me with a demanding insistence that sends shockwaves of pleasure through my core. My thighs clench reflexively around his hand, my back arching as I struggle to contain the sensation.

"Do you think about me?" he murmurs, his voice a low rumble that resonates through me, setting my nerve endings alight. His breath is warm against my temple, stirring the fine hairs there, each exhalation a tangible reminder of his proximity, his power over me. "When you touch yourself, do you moan my name?"

The truth spills from my lips without hesitation, a single, breathy syllable that holds the weight of my desire, my obsession. "Yes," I confess, any semblance of pride or self-preservation abandoned in the wake of his touch.

"Good." The word is a growl of pure masculine satisfaction, a sound that vibrates through me, claiming ownership of my pleasure, my body, my very soul.

It should bother me, this loss of control, this surrender to a man who holds the power to unravel me completely. This isn't right, a voice whispers in the back of my mind, a feeble protest that's swiftly drowned out by the thrum of my pulse in my ears. But the alcohol has turned my brain to mush, clouding my judgment, loosening my inhibitions. *Sure, Anne, blame the alcohol. As if you aren't mush anytime he touches you.*

The sensation of his fingers thrusting into me is exquisite agony, each stroke stoking the fire that's been simmering beneath my skin since the moment I first saw him. He's relentless, his fingers expertly curling, hitting that secret spot that makes my body arch and my breath hitch. I'm pressed against the door, my fingers scrabbling for purchase against the unyielding wood, as if I could somehow escape the overwhelming pleasure that's threatening to consume me.

His touch is rough, the pads of his fingers leaving a brand inside me that I know I'll feel long after this moment has passed. The raw intensity of it all forces a cry from my lips, a sound that's swallowed by his kiss. His mouth claims mine with a possessive fervor that leaves no room for doubt—I am his, completely and irrevocably. My cries of pleasure are muffled by the insistent pressure of his lips, transformed into moans that echo the desperate pounding of my heart.

The climax that tears through me is a force of nature, unstoppable and wild. It's a tempest that sweeps away all thought, all reason, leaving nothing but the searing heat of release. His teeth sink into the flesh of my shoulder at the height of it, the sharp sting of pain merging with the waves of pleasure, extending the ecstasy into an almost unbearable intensity. The sensation of his bite, the feel of his fingers still buried deep within me, it's all too much, and yet, I crave more. I want everything he has to give, this man who holds the power to unravel me with just a touch.

The moan that emerges is worse than a secret. It's my private shame. "William." It comes out before I can stop it, propelled by pleasure and a terrible fantasy where this man is more to me than my teacher.

He strokes me as I come down. My whole body shivers. I can't seem to stop. Even in the shelter of his embrace, made suddenly kind in the aftermath, my cheeks burn from shame. I didn't moan *Professor Stratford.*

William. Something I've never called him before now.

Something I never will again.

He sets me gently against the wall as he straightens my clothes. I'm unable to move, unable to help. I'm limp as he arranges me for the generic public, like a doll he's about to parade. Except he didn't have an orgasm. Why? He was hard against my stomach. I can still feel the imprint of him, burning hot beneath layers of silk and wool.

His dark gaze meets mine. "Now, I'm going to take you back to campus. Don't argue with me. And don't even look at another man in the bar. They're not going to help you. I will put you over my shoulder if I have to."

CHAPTER FOUR

Every Secret Place

THE WORLD SPINS as I stumble back into the Pinnacle bar, my arm looped through Stratford's, the world suddenly made bright. I squint from the sudden light change, trying to focus on the contours of alcoholic bottles lined up above the bar, but they dance and blur like a watercolor painting in the rain. My heart pounds from the recent climax. I can't shake the feeling of his fingers inside me, the raw, aching need he's stoked to a fever pitch.

"Where's Daisy?"

Stratford's grip tightens on my arm, steadying me. Or holding me down in case I try to bolt. "She's gone. And I'm not going to knock on every door of the hotel looking for her, so she'll have to meet you back at the dorm."

"She wouldn't leave me with you." Though you never really know with Daisy. She might have gone upstairs with a man. Or she might have already left the hotel, off to more mysterious doings. She has her own secrets, her own ways of coping with the pressures of her life. "She knows I hate you."

"Is that why my hand still smells like you?"

Ignoring the flash of heat, I yank my arm away from him. "You're an asshole. I'm not leaving without my friend. She might be in trouble. You know, like she was last time when the Shakespeare Society kidnapped and almost killed her. You remember the Society, right? Yeah, of course you do. You led them before, and you're helping them now."

Hearing him admit that in the Provost house hurt.

Though hearing him tell me I was nothing but a *cute little co-ed* to pass the time felt worse.

"Don't talk about them." His tone holds warning.

Because he's protecting them.

"Right. Secret societies do prefer to stay secret. It's kind of a core feature. Especially helpful when they plan to hurt students."

"Daisy's fine," he says, his voice gentling. "And you're fine. I'm going to take you back to Hathaway. She'll show up at some point. And you'll both be hungover tomorrow. Sound good?"

I look down to hide the disappointment that's surely on my face. Part of me wanted to deny it. After all, if he came here to protect me, then he can't be part of them. Instead he told me to not even speak their name. "Fine."

He leads me to the drive with its gold-and-black-felt luggage carts lined up. A few bills pressed into the hand of one of the bellmen, and a taxi appears in front of us. The old-fashioned kind. Not even an Uber.

Despite our harsh words, he's a gentleman about making sure I don't trip or wobble as I get into the back seat. Or maybe he just thinks I'm drunk enough to fall over. I wish. Unfortunately, I'm sober enough to realize how much this feels like a date would be, if we were just two regular people instead of a professor and student. He climbs in on the other side with a terse, "The university," for the driver.

Then we're off, alone in the dark space, lights whizzing by, the scent of his cologne wrapping around me. The ride isn't particularly smooth. The cabbie possibly learned to drive in a video game. He pulls a little hard at the turns, and I find myself leaning into Professor Stratford, my hand grazing the rough stubble on his jaw, my heart doing a tipsy tango in my chest. It's hard to remember why I'm supposed to fear him when he holds me like I'm something precious to him.

"You know, for a stuffy professor, you clean up pretty well." I probably shouldn't admit that, but the whiskey runs through my veins. It makes me honest. Always dangerous, being honest.

"Thanks. Maybe I'll add that to my CV." Despite his curt words, there's an undercurrent of something else, something that mirrors the electricity zapping between us with every accidental touch.

"Why so grumpy, Professor?" I ask, my voice teasing.

He shifts beside me, the streetlights casting shadows across his stern face. "I'm not grumpy," he says, but his clipped tone betrays him. It's more than being stuffy or grumpy, actually. It's almost like he's in pain.

I tilt my head, pretending to ponder, then a realization dawns on me. My eyes widen, and I lean in closer, my voice dropping to a conspiratorial whisper. "Ohhhhh, I know why you're upset."

He raises an eyebrow. "Enlighten me, Ms. Hill."

I bite my lip to stifle a giggle, then let my hand drift over to his lap, feeling the hardened bulge beneath the fabric of his slacks. "It's because you didn't get to come," I say, my voice husky as I trace the outline of his erection with my fingers.

He inhales sharply, a rough sound escaping his throat as he tenses under my touch. But he doesn't push me away. Instead, he stares forward in the cab, his Adam's apple bobbing as he swallows.

I take that as an invitation. No, more than that. I take it as him basically *begging* me, and if that's how strongly he feels about it? Well, then maybe I'll just keep rubbing him, my movements lazy, each stroke fanning the flames of that supply closet. His breathing comes harder, and even though he's not touching me, mine does, too. The cab is filled with the silent symphony of our suppressed desires, the hum of the engine keeping time.

He turns to look at me then, his brown eyes dark and intense, a silent battle waging behind them. But he remains still, trapped between propriety and the raw, animalistic need that I've so shamelessly laid bare. The tension between us is palpable, a living thing that threatens to consume us both.

His hand clamps down over mine, stopping the motion but not pulling it away. "Anne," he murmurs, his voice a low growl that sends shivers down my spine. "We can't."

I look up at him, and I'm sure he can see the want in them, the need that's clawing at my insides, begging for release. "But you want to," I whisper, my voice barely audible over the sound of the cabbie's music playing softly on the radio. "And more importantly, I want to."

He shakes his head, a small, almost imperceptible movement, but his resolve is clear. "No. Not here." His words are firm, but there's a ragged edge to his voice that betrays him. He's struggling, fighting against the tide of desire that's threatening to sweep us both away.

I bite my lip, feeling a twinge of disappointment, but there's also a thrill that courses through me, knowing that I have this effect on him. I lean closer, my lips grazing the shell of his ear. "Tell me," I breathe, my voice a sultry whisper. "Tell me what you wish you could do to me right now."

For a moment, he doesn't respond, and I wonder if I've pushed too far, if he'll shut down and retreat behind the wall of propriety he's so carefully constructed. But then he murmurs into my ear, his words soft but potent, his voice a low rumble that sends shivers down my spine.

"I would start by tracing the curve of your neck with my lips, exploring every inch of you until you're arching into my touch, desperate for more. I'd let my hands wander, relearn the softness of your skin." A soft, almost self-deprecating chuckle. "I've never been able to forget the way your breasts look. Or the way your hips feel in my hands while I'm fucking you."

I feel my cheeks heat at his boldness, but I can't deny the thrill that races through me, igniting a fire that I've kept carefully banked.

"I'd use my mouth to worship you, to taste every secret place until you're crying out my name, until you belong to me, until you're mine."

His words intoxicate me more than the whiskey could. I'm lost in the fantasy, imagining his powerful hands and skilled mouth. It's a dangerous game we're playing, but in this moment, I'm powerless to resist.

"When you've come again and again, when you're tender, too sensitive, that's when I'd shove my cock inside you. You'd squirm and cry out and tell me it was too much, but that would only drive me on. I'd only go harder."

Each word feels like a caress, igniting a fire that burns low in my belly. I can feel myself getting wetter with every filthy promise, my body aching for him to make good on his words. It's wickedly erotic, the two of us sitting there in the back of the cab, exchanging hushed, heated whispers while the world goes on around us, oblivious.

The cabbie seems to be lost in his own world, his focus on the road ahead, but I'm acutely aware of his presence, just a few feet away. It adds an edge to our illicit exchange, the thrill of the forbidden, the danger of being caught.

It's deliciously naughty.

Stratford's hand is still over mine, pressing me against him, and I can feel him getting thicker, pulsing with arousal. He's so hard beneath my fingers, and I know he's on the edge, just as much as I am. But he's right, we can't do this here, not with the cabbie just a few feet away. So, I settle for the next best thing, keeping my hand exactly where it is, feeling the evidence of his need for me, and I revel in the knowledge that I'm the one who's done this to him.

When we get close to the university, Stratford directs the driver to turn right and then left. And then stop right here. We're pulled up the shortest distance from Hathaway. Any closer and we'd have to pass through one of the little security booths on the major intersections. Cars can only get through if a passenger has a school ID, and even they can't park without a permit.

Stratford pays the driver and helps me step out, where cold night air hits me like a thousand tiny nips. The ride had been a sparkly, sensual dream wrapped around us. It felt so good, the sense of freedom, of boldness, the way he responded to me.

Stepping out of the cab onto the familiar, yet suddenly alien terrain of campus, it's like a splash of cold water. Hathaway Dormitory looms ahead, its grim, dilapidated façade a stark contrast to the opulence of the Pinnacle.

I take a step forward, and my heel catches on the curb, sending me lurching forward. My heart leaps into my throat, and for a moment, I'm sure I'm going to face-plant right here on the sidewalk. But then strong arms are around me, pulling me back against him, his grip firm.

I let out a little giggle, embarrassment mingling with relief. "Whoa, that was close," I say, my voice sounding too loud in the quiet night.

Stratford mutters a curt, "Fuck," under his breath, but he doesn't let go. Instead, he holds me until I'm steady, his body a solid, comforting presence.

"Thanks for the…ride," I say, the double

entendre taking me by surprise, and I giggle again. Damn it, I *never* giggle. Why tonight?

Stratford grunts. "Let's go."

"Umm, what? No. You can't come with me." The walls of Tanglewood University might be thick, but the rumors spread like wildfire.

"Watch me."

"Someone might see. Us. Together." I gesture broadly at the darkened buildings with the occasional lighted window winking at us. "Besides, I know the way to the dorm. It's like, right there."

Stratford's eyes narrow, his voice dropping to a low, annoyed rumble. "I have to come with you or else you'd fall on your face."

"That's not true." I draw myself up, trying to project an air of sober condescendence. "And even if it were, we're close enough that I could crawl there."

"That's not as reassuring as you might think it is." He interrupts me when I open my mouth to argue. "I'm coming. The sooner you accept that, the sooner this is over."

"Fine."

I'm acutely aware of the space between us, the way our bodies seem to move in sync, despite the awkwardness of the situation. I can't help but feel a twinge of disappointment. The night is coming to an end, and with it, the fantasy that's been sustaining me. I know that once I step through those doors, the spell will be broken, and I'll be Cinderella surrounded by pumpkin detritus.

We reach the double-door entrance to Hathaway. I turn to face him, the frosty night air making me acutely aware of the warmth that's been radiating from his body. "Well, good night."

"Keep going."

"We're already here."

"Yes, we're here at a dorm full of drunk, stupid, violent college boys who could drag you into their dorm room before you can blink. I'm walking you to your room."

"Those drunk, stupid, violent college boys have eyes, and we can't be seen together. You're a professor. I'm a student."

"Perhaps you can say it even louder, so everyone can hear."

"You are so stubborn," I say, hating that it makes me hot.

His lips curl, as if he can read the desire on my skin. Maybe he can. Maybe it's written in that old-fashioned scrawl that's tattooed across his muscled abdomen, saying *Anne likes it when you're a big, commanding asshole.*

Without a word, I whirl and head to the elevator bank.

He follows, thankfully not saying a word.

Despite our fears of random college boys, the dorm is eerily quiet. It's like the whole building is holding its breath, waiting for something to happen.

On the third floor, I fumble with the key, my fingers clumsy and uncoordinated. He takes it from me, unlocking the door. The door swings open, revealing the tiny chaos of our room. It's empty, of course.

I collapse onto my bed with a long, drawn-out sigh. The sheets are cool against my flushed skin, and I fan out my arms as if I'm making a snow angel. I'm horizontal now, safe from any prying eyes or dangerous hands, but Stratford doesn't leave.

Instead he steps inside, allowing the door to close behind him.

CHAPTER FIVE
This Fucking Scholar

HE WANDERS AROUND the room, his movements slow and deliberate, as if he's trying to memorize every detail. He picks up a book from the floor, studying the cover. "*Advanced Theoretical Mechanics and Structural Dynamics*," he reads aloud.

I prop myself up on my elbow. "Don't. It's so boring you would die."

His lips quirk. "My brother wrote this."

Shit. "What I meant was—"

"I agree with you."

I grin at him like an idiot. "Is it weird having a brother who likes…" My voice drops to a whisper, as if I'm saying an evil word. Which I kind of am. "Math?"

"He was strange in our household. My father studied Shakespeare. And then me. Asher was always fiddling with one instrument or another.

Only Cormac took after our mother that way, but she was across the ocean."

"You never saw her?"

"It was better when we didn't." He picks up a framed photo from my desk and studies it. Rusty is my dog, and the main thing I miss when I'm at school. "You two look happy."

"He'd just chased a squirrel into the lake that day, so he was happy."

"What about you?"

"I'm not that fast of a runner."

He gives me a slow, devastating smile. He sets the photo down, his gaze lingering on it for a moment longer before he moves on to where, unfortunately, I have the original black-and-gold invitation pinned to the wall.

He runs a forefinger over the embossed skull design.

The same finger he used inside me an hour before.

It's wrong in every way, but there's something about the way he handles my things, the way he makes himself at home in our little world, that sends a thrill coursing through me. "You should get some sleep," he says, his voice husky. "It's been a long night."

"Stay," I murmur, the word slipping out before I can stop it.

Why did I say that? Even as I berate myself, I can't take it back. The room is cold without him. So empty. His vibrance makes everything more interesting, more full, more sweet. It's the terrible truth about him.

"I don't belong with you," he says, and the most surface, most scared part of me thinks, of course he doesn't. He belongs with someone beautiful and wealthy, someone who doesn't need to be rescued.

That part of me has been muted by the whiskey. It's still there, but the volume has been turned down. Instead, I'm able to hear something even better. Something Shakespeareans love the most: subtext.

He says, *I don't belong with you,* and the subtext, the undertone, the literary analysis of those words means, *I'm too dangerous, too old, too stuffy for you.*

Exactly as I'd accused him in the taxi.

They weren't a lie, either.

Maybe I wouldn't normally have said them, but nothing about tonight is normal. He's all those things, but I want him anyway.

"Why *were* you at that hotel?" I ask again, almost knowing the answer, even though it defies belief, even though it's impossible.

I might as well believe in ghosts telling me that my father's murderer was my uncle, like Hamlet, but why not? Why not think unthinkable things? The magic of black ink and flipping pages feels prescient in the room.

"Don't." But even as he says it, he draws closer.

I sit up as his hungry gaze moves over my body. "Tell me."

He hesitates, glancing at the door before returning to me. For a moment, I think he's going to say no, to leave me alone in the quiet darkness. Alone. Alone. Alone. The way I've always been, really.

His eyes are dark, unreadable, but the tension in his body mirrors my own. "Anne," he says, his voice a low warning. "This is madness."

It's a madness we both crave, a fire that burns too hot to deny. I stand and press my lips to his in a desperate, hungry kiss. For a moment, he resists, and then he's kissing me back, furious and tender, possessing and possessed.

"Tell me," I repeat in a whisper.

"I've had you watched," he says, the words torn from the tarnished center of him. "Stalked, basically. Is that what you wanted to hear? I have you followed while you're walking your dog on long rambles going nowhere. While some asshole tries to cop a feel while you pour his coffee. You should have poured it onto his lap, by the way."

"It was tempting."

"I knew the exact moment when you got to campus. And when you left with Ms. Bradshaw, all dressed up, I knew exactly where you were going."

"You followed us there."

A rough laugh. "I left in the middle of an important pre-semester dinner with other professors, probably sounding like a madman, coming up with some half-formed excuse, because I couldn't tell them, there's no way I could tell them I was going to see a student about sex."

About sex.

I should be appalled, of course. Society is quite clear on this. I should shove him away and scream and maybe even call the police. That's what young women are supposed to do when faced with a stalker. But society doesn't have anything to say about parents who hit you, parents who lie, parents who just need a few dollars for medicine, my God, Anne, why are you so selfish?

About sex.

Society doesn't have anything to say about working so damn hard so that the magic carpet of academia can take me away, only to find myself still wanting, still needing, still so damn alone it feels like a physical ache.

Society can go to hell.

About sex.

"Do it," I whisper, my lips inches away from his chest, at the V where the white dress shirt opens, revealing the tanned hollow of his throat, a vulnerable point on a strong man. "Do what you told me in the taxi."

He groans, this articulate man. This professor of literature. This author. This fucking scholar. He's become wordless.

We're a tangle of limbs and clothing, shedding layers as we stumble towards my bed. The thin mattress creaks under our combined weight, but I don't care. All that matters is the feel of his skin against mine, the taste of his kiss, the way he makes me feel alive.

His hands roam over my body, mapping out every curve and hollow. I arch into his touch, my fingers digging into the muscles of his back. We move together in a dance as old as time, our bodies speaking a language all their own.

I can feel the weight of his gaze on me, a tangible force that sets my skin alight. He's watching me with an intensity that borders on predatory, and yet, I feel no fear. Only a deep, aching need that throbs in time with my heartbeat.

"I would start by tracing the curve of your neck with my lips," he'd said, and now he's fulfilling that promise. His mouth is a whisper against my skin, a ghostly touch that sends shivers cascading down my spine. He explores me with a reverence that's both humbling and empowering, his lips charting a path from my jawline to the sensitive spot where my pulse flutters wildly.

I can't help but arch into his touch, my body moving of its own accord. I'm desperate for more, for the feel of his hands on me, and he doesn't disappoint. His fingers skim over my shoulders, down my arms, leaving a trail of goose bumps in their wake. He's relearning the softness of my skin, his touch a mixture of tenderness and command that leaves me breathless.

He pulls me closer, his hands settling on my hips, and I can feel the evidence of his arousal pressing against me. It's a heady reminder of the power I hold over him, a power that's both thrilling and terrifying. He's a man of intellect and control, and yet, with me, he's unraveling, his carefully constructed façade slipping away to reveal the raw, primal need beneath.

His lips find mine in a kiss that's both a question and a demand. I open myself to him, our tongues dancing in a sensual rhythm that mirrors the ebb and flow of our bodies. He tastes of whiskey and something darker, something that speaks of late nights and forbidden desires.

I'd let my hands wander, relearn the softness of your skin.

His hands roam freely over my body, cupping my breasts, teasing my nipples into hard peaks. I gasp into his mouth, the sensation sending jolts of pleasure straight to my core. He breaks the kiss, his eyes dark with desire as he watches my reaction to his touch.

"You're so responsive," he murmurs, his voice a low growl that vibrates through me. "So beautiful when you let go."

I can feel myself blushing at his words, but there's no time for embarrassment. He's moving lower, his lips blazing a trail of fire down my neck, over my collarbone, to the valley between my breasts. He worships my body with his mouth, his hands, his very presence, and I'm lost in a sea of sensation, adrift in a world where only he and I exist.

I've never been able to forget the way your breasts

look. Or the way your hips feel in my hands while I'm fucking you.

He hooks his fingers into the waistband of my panties, his gaze never leaving mine as he slowly peels them away. There's a promise in his eyes, a dark, delicious promise that makes my heart race with anticipation.

"Spread your legs for me," he murmurs.

I do as he says, my body obeying before my mind has fully processed the command. He settles between my thighs, his breath hot against my most intimate parts. I'm exposed and vulnerable, but I've never felt safer, never felt more desired.

He looks up at me, his eyes locked on mine as he slowly, deliberately, runs his tongue over me. The sensation is electric, a bolt of lightning that courses through my veins, setting my nerves alight. I can't help but cry out, my hands fisting the sheets as he explores me with a thoroughness that leaves no part untouched.

He's relentless, his mouth and tongue working in tandem to drive me to the brink of madness. I'm a symphony of moans and gasps, each note drawn from the deepest part of me, each breath a testament to the pleasure he's wringing from my body.

"Please," I say, not knowing what I'm asking

for, only that I need more, need him, need the release that's hovering just out of reach.

He answers my plea with a low chuckle, the vibrations sending me spiraling closer to the edge. "Patience, dear heart."

And with that, he plunges two fingers inside me, curling them in a way that makes my back arch off the bed. He's everywhere, his fingers and mouth working in unison to drive me wild, to shatter me into a thousand pieces.

I'm teetering on the precipice, my body wound tight with need, when he suddenly stops, pulling back to look at me with a wicked glint in his eye.

"You know what I need," he says, his voice a dark whisper that sends a shiver down my spine. "What I want. And you're going to give it to me."

I'm left panting, my body aching for completion.

My brain fumbles with the scratchy, sepia-toned tape of *the cab ride.*

I'd use my mouth to worship you, to taste every secret place until you're crying out my name, until you belong to me, until you're mine.

The words slip from my lips, a surrender of sorts, even though the implications of them terrify me. "William, please. I'm yours."

It's a declaration, a plea, and a promise all wrapped into one.

He growls in response, the sound vibrating through me, and then his mouth is on me again, his lips closing around my clit with a suction that feels like a direct line to my soul. The sensation is too much, too intense, and I cry out, "William," loud enough for anyone on the floor to hear.

Orgasm hits me like a freight train, my body convulsing under the onslaught of pleasure. It's endless, wave after wave crashing over me, reforming me into someone else, a creature of need and sensation. The words echo in my mind, *I'm his now. His. Forever.* It's a terrifying thought, and yet, in this moment of vulnerability and ecstasy, it feels right.

I collapse onto the bed, a boneless, panting mess, as he continues to lick me gently, his touch soothing now, rather than demanding. I'm floating, adrift in a sea of bliss, my body humming with satisfaction.

With tender movements, he pulls my dress down, covering my exposed skin, and then he's rearranging my limbs, positioning me so that I'm lying properly in the bed. I feel like a doll in his hands, limp, utterly at his mercy.

His gaze lingers on me, a possessive gleam in

his eyes that sends a shiver down my spine. "Sleep now," he murmurs.

My body's already succumbing to the dark sea, lulled by his steady dark gaze, the echoes of my orgasm. Except it's not time for that. "But you said that—" I stammer, too embarrassed to speak clearly, my words made slow and drawled from the echoes of orgasm. "You said that you would shove your—That after you would—"

"Go on," he says, his eyes glittering.

When you've come again and again, when you're tender, too sensitive, that's when I'd shove my cock inside you. You'd squirm and cry out and tell me it was too much, but that would only drive me on. I'd only go harder.

"You said you wouldn't stop."

He presses a kiss, almost chaste, to my forehead, as if I'm a small child and he's tucking me in. "That was a fantasy, Anne. It was a dream. In real life, I'm a predator, and you're the prey. Stay away from me. Push me away if you want to save yourself, because the next time I see you, I'm fucking that beautiful mouth."

CHAPTER SIX

A Real Ball Buster

I SLIP INTO the lecture hall, the hushed whispers of past lectures still echoing in the air. The room is overly warm, ancient heaters not knowing when to stop, a stark contrast to the chill I've left behind outside. I choose a seat near the front, like usual.

I've never been the kind of girl to sit in the back row, to scroll on my phone during class, to flirt with boys instead of studying. Which makes the red whisker burn on my neck more embarrassing.

Why did I let him do that?

You didn't let *him, Anne. You begged for him.*

I wish I could blame the whiskey, but the truth is I feel the desire even now, stone-cold sober. Part of me wants to believe he's good. And he protected me, didn't he? I would feel far more regret if I'd slept with Grandpa.

My fingers trace the grooves on the desk surface, carved by years of students like me, all chasing dreams and dodging nightmares.

Students like William Stratford, once upon a time. The Shakespeare Society's shadow looms over him, a dark specter that whispers of danger and deceit. I can't shake the image of him, entangled in their web, the thought turning my stomach.

I pull out my notes, the pages filled with scribbles and highlights, a testament to my determination. Literature, my beacon in the storm, my escape from the lies and abuse back home, even if it means leaving Rusty behind. I won't be another statistic, another casualty of my parents' dysfunction.

Shakespeare's words are my solace, a reminder that there's beauty and truth in this world, even if it's hidden among thoughtless violence.

The hall begins to fill with the bustle of arriving students.

A familiar presence plops down next to me: Tyler, with his disheveled curly hair and energy drink sweatshirt that looks like it's survived a few too many late-night study sessions.

"Anne, my man," he greets, his voice a blend of enthusiasm and the subtle undercurrent of mischief. "Ready for a new semester of Shakespeare and keg parties?"

I can't help but smile back, his energy infectious. "Not so much with the parties, for me. I'm gonna focus on school this time."

He snorts. "This time? That's every time. Come on. You can't live in the books. Life's too short not to enjoy the footnotes."

"You have a gift for making things seem lighter."

Tyler's grin fades into a look of genuine concern, his dark eyes softening. "Did you have a rough winter break?"

Rough? Mmm, maybe. More like heartbreaking.

It's hard to pretend that my mom has cancer now that I know the truth. It's also hard to look the other way when they demand money for her treatment. The sad truth is she probably does need treatment. The mental kind. But none of the money I earned from the diner will go towards that.

"Family," I say, unable to explain.

"Yeah, I know the feeling."

"You do? It's hard to imagine anyone having a problem with you."

He nudges my arm. "Stop. I'm going to think

you have a crush on me."

I roll my eyes at his teasing. "Whatever."

"*We didn't move to this country for you to read poems.*" He mimics an accent and a high pitch. "*Why don't you become a doctor like your cousin? He's going to be able to support his mother in her old age, not like you.*"

I wince. "That sucks."

"That's why I like to have fun. To make up for the rest of it."

The lecture hall fills with the hum of conversation and the scraping of chair legs against the floor. Maybe, just maybe, I can manage to keep my head on straight this semester—between the pages of Shakespeare. And absolutely not in the allure of the Shakespeare Society's parties. Or the magnetic pull of one particular professor.

The *fun* thing may work for Tyler.

I've already proven I can't be trusted with it.

"If we're going to a tragedy," he says, "at least it's a real one this semester. *Hamlet* is gonna rock, but like in a super depressing, mentally unstable way."

I can't help but bristle at his words. "Seriously?"

"I know Professor Stratford tried to sell the whole female agency thing, but, like, at the end of the day they're just two teenagers in love." When he sees my narrow eyes, he amends. "I mean, one teenager. We don't know Romeo's age."

"He's not the point." Lots of scholars dismiss *Romeo and Juliet*, seeing only reckless young love. "Women in Shakespeare's time didn't have many choices, but that makes the ones they made even more important."

Professor Stratford understood that.

At least I thought so.

I'm not supposed to be thinking of him either way.

"Right, right, right," Tyler says, clearly trying to placate the crazy feminist Shakespearean. "She was great. It's just... Hamlet's a heavier hitter, you know? The questions he grapples with—they're timeless."

Ugh. Saying that women's choices *aren't* timeless is freaking sexist. But I force myself to focus on Tyler's enthusiasm for *Hamlet*. After all, it is a masterpiece of its own. I can appreciate the complexity of its characterization, but part of me—a stubborn, defiant part—refuses to let go of Juliet's narrative.

"I'm not only excited about *Hamlet*," he says, a mischievous glint in his eye. "There's something else that's great about this semester."

"Oh?" I ask, bracing myself for whatever comes next. Tyler has a knack for surprises, though usually, they're harmless—like the time he convinced half the class to attend a play in Elizabethan attire.

"Professor Isolde Thorne," he says, as if revealing a grand secret.

"She's listed on the class schedule."

"Yeah, but did you know she's hot," he finishes, his eyebrows dancing suggestively. "Like really fuckable, especially for a professor."

The blood drains from my face at hearing the words *fuckable* and *professor* in the same sentence. Is it possible Tyler knows about Stratford and me?

No, of course not. I'm being paranoid.

Tyler continues, oblivious to my discomfort, his gaze busy fantasizing about whatever faculty picture he probably jerked off to. "She's got that sexy-librarian vibe down."

"I dare you to say it to her face."

"Absolutely not," he says. "I hear she's a real ball buster."

I hide my sigh. Reducing an accomplished professor to her physical appearance. Calling a woman a *ball buster* when a man would get labeled *tough but fair*. It's a stark reminder of a world where my worth is often measured by my fuckability rather than the quality of my work.

Was that why Stratford had sex with me?

Was I just another conquest, a notch on his academic belt?

The thought stings, a sharp contrast to the fleeting warmth I felt in his arms.

Professor Stratford was a storm I willingly walked into, fully aware of the damage it could cause. I have to be smarter than the men who would see me as nothing more than an object of desire.

Dr. Isolde Thorne is a force to be reckoned with in the world of Shakespearean academia. Maybe she can be a role model for me.

She strides into the lecture hall. Conversations die down, chairs creak as students sit up a little straighter, and the air grows heavy with anticipation.

Her presence commands the room, though she's not much taller than me. She strides to the podium with a confident grace. She wears high black heels, a no-nonsense black pencil skirt, a loose-sleeved white button-down. A wide black silk tie at her neck provides a blend of both seriousness and femininity. Her black hair is pulled back into a high bun.

I can't help but acknowledge the truth in

Tyler's assessment. Yes, Professor Thorne is attractive, but it's so much more than that. She carries herself with authority. And she exudes a "don't fuck with me" attitude that I'm desperate to emulate.

As she sets her leather bag on the podium, her dark eyes scan the room, daring anyone to challenge her. The silence is deafening, a testament to the respect she inspires. Or is it fear? Her gaze lands on me for a brief moment, and I feel a jolt of adrenaline. It's like she can see right through me.

I sit up taller, meeting her gaze with a determined one of my own.

"*Fulbright Fellow*," she says, her tone matter-of-fact. "Recipient of the Early Career Researcher award. My work has been published in the most prestigious Shakespearean journals." She pauses, allowing the weight of her words to settle over the room. "The National Endowment for the Humanities funds my work. Why do I say this? Because I'm the best. You all are fortunate to learn from someone of my caliber."

Her gaze sweeps across the room, daring anyone to question her qualifications. I can't help but raise my eyebrows, duly impressed. This is not a woman who shyly accepts accolades; she wears them like battle armor, polished and proud.

"You will keep your phones off," she continues, her voice a lash of cold precision. "You will arrive on time and turn in your work when it's due. Fail to adhere to these simple rules, and you might as well remove yourself from my classroom. I don't care whether you like me. Or whether other professors like me. I'm here for the work. For the study. For Shakespeare."

Her words hang in the air, a stark warning that leaves no room for misunderstanding. I find myself sitting taller, a spark of admiration igniting within me.

"Holy shit," Tyler mutters beside me.

He doesn't sound mad. He sounds turned on.

That is the kind of power I aspire to—unapologetic, unwavering, and undeniably earned. Professor Thorne isn't just a teacher; she's a trailblazer, carving out a space for herself in a field dominated by men.

This is what I need to be.

Which means no more mooning over Professor Stratford.

She launches into the syllabus, outlining the expectations for the semester ahead. I'm struck by a sense of clarity. This is my chance to prove myself, to show that I'm more than just a girl from a shitty town with a troubled past. I am a scholar, a thinker, a contender in the world of Shakespearean literature.

Like her.

"In addition to your regular coursework this semester, each of you will have the opportunity to compete for the prestigious Tempest Prize." She pauses, letting her words sink in. "It's awarded to an exceptional student in the field of Shakespearean literature, someone who demonstrates a profound understanding of the Bard's work and contributes an original interpretation."

My breath catches in my throat. The Tempest Prize could be my ticket to a future where my intellect is recognized, where my analysis of Shakespeare's work might shine alongside that of other aspiring scholars.

"The prize includes a substantial cash prize, though the honor you receive as the recipient will help you far more in your academic career than any dollar amount."

Just how substantial is this cash prize? Enough that I can buy my own textbooks without needing to visit the Pinnacle, I'm guessing. That alone makes it worth winning. It's not something I would confess out loud, because it would seem mercenary. As if I didn't care about the art, which isn't true. I care a lot about the art, but it doesn't come cheaply.

Murmurs ripple over the classroom, but her voice cuts through.

"I will personally mentor one student," she says. "Together, we will craft an interpretation that has the potential to win you this esteemed award."

I exchange a glance with Tyler, who looks excited at the idea of spending alone time with Professor Thorne. Of course, everyone wants to win an exclusive mentorship. It would be a huge advantage. Her gaze lands on me for a fraction of a second longer, and I wonder if she sees the eagerness in my eyes.

"Your mentor relationship with me," she continues, "won't be based solely on your past academic achievements or your family name—no, I care about none of that." She smiles in a cool, feline way. "I am going to select my protégé based on merit, right here, right now. You'll have sixty seconds to impress me."

Energy surges through the classroom, through me.

Shakespearean study isn't an area known for its speed. No, we agonize over every single word. It takes years. Decades. Centuries, even.

Instead, we have a single minute.

"Give me your best analysis of Ophelia's madness." Sixty seconds to prove our worth in a frenzy of scribbled notes. Insane. She's daring us to rise to the occasion. "Ready?" she asks, her voice devoid of warmth. "Set. Go."

The lecture hall erupts into motion as students scramble for paper and pencils. My heart pounds as I weave together a few sentences that are insightful and representative of my work. Seconds tick by with breathtaking speed, each one increasing the pressure of this crucial chance to impress.

The scratch of pencils on paper.

The rhythmic tap of Professor Thorne's foot.

The tick, tick, tick of the clock.

Those are the only sounds in the lecture hall.

"Time's up," she says. "Pencils down."

Writing stops, the air heavy with anticipation.

"Let's find out what insights you've crafted for me," she says, gesturing for the girl in the bottom right. "Read them aloud."

Many of them sound like they could have been quoting CliffsNotes. Ophelia's insanity is due to the grief of her father's death. Pain over Hamlet's betrayal of her. Frustration in a cruel court. They're valid but also unoriginal, and

Professor Thorne's cool gaze reflects her feelings about that.

Then we get to Matteo. The overhead lights catch the subtle highlights in his silky hair. His eyes, a deep, espresso brown, scan the room. Then he smiles at Professor Thorne, revealing a dimple.

His voice a rich baritone that fills the room. "Laertes is moved by her madness, making her lunacy not only a symptom of the darkness, but the precursor. A woman could not wield a sword, but her actions still led to avenge her father's death. Would Laertes even have murdered Hamlet, if not for her characterization?"

Damn. That's actually an interesting argument.

Bold. Fresh. New, but with enough text to draw a compelling case.

I recognize him from the Shakespeare Society party last semester, but I've never actually met him. Somehow our classes have never overlapped. It's clear he's not just a pretty face. He's a force to be reckoned with. And he could have won this little game with those two sentences.

"Very nice, Mr. Andini," she says, and he nods his head in acceptance of her praise, an academic prince accepting his due.

The readings continue, though my mind

remains on Matteo's. It's an interesting phrase, but it also paints Ophelia as a victim of circumstance rather than an active player in her life. Then again, we can't ignore the real results of trauma. I'm torn on the subject, wanting to understand Ophelia's pain and yet also wanting her to mean more than that.

My pulse speeds up as we reach my row.

Tyler goes before me. He grins at the class. "Ophelia's lunacy parallels the chaos and cruelty of the Danish court…like Pinky's antics inside the cage of a science lab. Brain, of course, is Hamlet."

Laughter and snorts break out.

I can't help but smile at his audacity.

Professor Thorne's expression hardens. "Shakespeare is not a joke."

Chastened, Tyler sinks into his chair.

Shit. Shakespeare may be a cornerstone of English literature, but he loved comedy. Slapstick. Dirty jokes. Nothing was off-limits. He wove humor into his plays as deftly as he did tragedy. How can we appreciate the full spectrum of his genius if we don't acknowledge the comedic side?

I want to reassure Tyler, but I'm busy freaking out.

Because it's my turn.

Deep breath.

My hand trembles, so I press it flat against the desk.

"Ophelia's madness has been described as a rebellion against her harsh reality, but I would go a step further and say that it's a series of symptoms that can be directly tied to complex PTSD. In other words, it's a trauma response."

Professor Thorne's eyebrows rise. "Very nice."

It's only then that I realize that my argument is in direct opposition to Matteo's. He paints her as the prop used to motivate men, aka the real characters.

I can't help adding: "She's more than a catalyst for men."

My breath hitches on a surge of pride at the small gesture. As the class finishes reading, I can only hope it's enough.

When the last student speaks, Professor Thorne's gaze sweeps over us. My heart beats wildly in my chest. The tension in the room creates a silent symphony. She's silent for a moment, her eyes lingering on each face, each hopeful expression. *Say Anne,* I think, focusing on her red lips. I wish I was like Matilda from the old Roald Dahl book, someone able to move things with her mind, able to change her world from the force of will alone.

"There was some thoughtful, fresh, insightful commentary. And some that barely scratched the surface. However, there is one that rose to the top. I'm pleased to announce that the student I'll be personally mentoring is…"

The blood rushes to my face, a mixture of anticipation and fear.

"…Matteo."

My heart sinks, a leaden weight in my chest. It's not that Matteo isn't deserving—his argument was compelling. Disappointment still stings.

Congratulations are offered to Matteo, his victory met with a mix of genuine admiration and thinly veiled envy. He has plenty of friends, though. There's an undeniable charm to the way he carries himself, a confident ease that draws attention without him even trying.

There's groaning from students, their disappointment a mirror of my own. We all wanted this.

Professor Thorne raises a hand, silencing the room with a single gesture. "Don't worry," she says. "You will all get mentors in the department, teaching assistants who will help you with your entries."

Her words are meant to be reassuring. But how can I hope to win a prize that spans the entire country if I couldn't even beat a single classroom?

The Tempest Prize feels impossibly out of reach.

CHAPTER SEVEN

Tempest Prize

THE BECKINSALE LIBRARY of Natural Science looms ahead, its grandeur a testament to its breadth of knowledge. I pause, taking in the sight of the iconic elephant statue standing guard at the entrance. Its dark copper surface has been rubbed to a bright shine on its toes, a tradition among the students who touch it for luck before exams or important projects.

I take some comfort in the ritual as I rub the bumps.

Daisy shakes her head. "Don't tell me you believe that?"

"Umm, hello, nice to meet you, Shakespeare person here. We believe in all portends, prophecies, and amulets."

"Remind me again why his stuff isn't stored in the English literature library. Oh wait, that's because you don't have one."

"Shut up." This is a sore spot for lit majors.

Beckinsale was an old guy who loved hunting shit in Africa, and he had a lot of money. So in thanks for his generous donation, it was given his name along with the term natural science. It houses most of the literature material, as well as sciences. Along with engineering, since they don't take up much space, preferring to keep things digital whenever possible.

It makes sense to me that books about Alan Turing would be shelved near Lewis Carroll, who was also a math professor. That Ada Lovelace would be shelved near Lord Byron, who was her father. The sciences and art have always danced together.

But I'm not about to tell her that.

Lit majors have a chip on our shoulder about this. It's practically a requirement.

We push through the heavy doors and step into the hushed interior of the library. The scent of old books and polished wood fills my senses, a familiar aroma that always seems to settle my nerves.

"Where are you headed?" she asks.

I check the meeting assignment on my phone. "Sixth floor."

"I'm heading to the basement. Have fun."

I take the elevator up. An extremely old, yellowed piece of paper has been taped to the wall since I got here. *Shhhhhhh,* it says, a glasses-wearing owl holding its feathered wing to its beak.

Always a surprise to see him there.

Seems like someone would take him down or at least draw something offensive over the top of it in Sharpie, but somehow he's still there every time, growing slightly older.

Will I know the teaching assistant who's assigned to mentor me?

I've met some of them, of course, since I'm on the tail end of my junior year, but not all of them. It's a large school. I can't help but feel a twinge of jealousy towards Matteo. He's smart, but he didn't need the extra help to win.

But I don't need Thorne's help to win the Tempest Prize.

I can do it on my own merits.

And whoever my mentor turns out to be, whatever teacher's assistant got assigned to me, they'll still be from one of the most renowned humanities departments in the country.

I can learn from anyone.

The elevator dings. The doors slide open.

And I step forward, prepared to enter Denmark.

The sixth floor of the library feels like a hidden sanctuary, deserted except for the soft hum of overhead lights. I pass towering shelves stuffed with well-worn tomes. The spines whisper stories as I run my fingers over them, the texture of leather and paper grounding me.

Wandering deeper into the stacks, I let the scent of aging paper and ink wash over me. Each step feels deliberate, almost reverent, as I navigate the labyrinth of literature. I reach the clearing of tables at the far end of the room, and my heart skips a beat.

Professor Stratford sits alone, surrounded by a spread of open books, his brow furrowed in concentration as he jots notes on a notepad. His dark hair, tousled and slightly curling at the ends, frames his face perfectly. The stubble on his jaw adds a rugged edge to his handsome features, making him look both scholarly and sexy as hell.

The ordinary library chair looks like a throne, the books his subjects beneath a powerful regard. He wears a crisp white shirt, sleeves rolled up to reveal toned forearms. Everything about him exudes confidence, from the way he holds his pen to the slight tilt of his head as he reads.

Worst of all, he's the only person here, which means that he must be my assigned mentor.

Surprise rushes through me, tinged with an uncomfortable amount of pleasure.

Damn it.

And also—of course. The universe seems determined to tempt me.

The silence wraps around me, almost suffocating, as I take a step closer. I still remember him touching me at the hotel, me touching him on the cab ride. My blood heats. Then there was what he did to me on the bed in my dorm. Am I really ready to face him after that? Of course I am. I'll be cool and confident and cosmopolitan.

I force myself to keep my voice steady. "So, I guess…you're my mentor?"

He glances up, his coffee-colored eyes unsurprised. "You didn't think you could avoid me forever, did you?"

The words come back to me in shocking vividness. *I'm a predator, and you're the prey. Stay away from me. Push me away if you want to save yourself, because the next time I see you, I'm fucking that beautiful mouth.*

"I thought you were going to be a TA."

"I'm not."

Wariness feels like an extra-caffeinated soda, tickling my nose. "Did you arrange this?"

"Arranged what, exactly?" he asks, toying with

the pen in his hand.

"Being my mentor. Did you ask them to assign me to you?"

"Yes," he says, his tone mocking. "I've been panting after you, unable to sleep or eat or do anything because I'm so desperate to fuck you again. Except, of course, that you're the one with your nipples hard, your cheeks flushed."

I feel my cheeks burn, and I regret ever having let him touch me. I'm mortified that he knows how much I wanted him, how much I still want him. "Listen, I'm not sure this is going to work out, considering our…history. I'll go get a different mentor."

"They already have their own assignments. They're too busy to take on someone else. But I suppose if you want to bother everyone, go ahead."

I open my mouth to argue, but I realize he's right. Complaining will just cause stress. And it will make me look like an absolute idiot to turn down one of the best Shakespeare scholars in the country. Anyone would kill for this opportunity. He has more experience, more publications, more renown than Professor Thorne.

So…this is a good thing. I swallow hard, trying to regain my composure. He can help me with my submission. It doesn't have to mean anything.

Nothing has to happen.

"Maybe you're worried because you want me to kiss you again," he says.

"Absolutely not."

His laugh is husky. "Or maybe you want me to make you come again. The sounds you make are so sweet…but then again, the library doesn't allow moans or whimpers or screaming my name, no matter how hard they make me."

Why is that so hot? "This is about the Tempest Prize," I say, my voice firm. "Not about whatever…personal business was between us."

His lips quirk. "Ah yes, the prestigious Tempest Prize. I bet Isolde talked it up quite a bit. Gave you a nice song and dance about how it would help your academic careers, the grand honor, et cetera, et cetera."

I flush, feeling the heat creeping up my neck. "Professor Thorne told us the truth about it," I say, my voice steady. "And she deserves your respect. So back off, or I will go to the dean."

Surprise. I can see calculations in his eyes, but he shrugs. "So, are we going to talk about your *Hamlet* analysis or should I continue my own work?"

I pull out my notes, trying to ignore the way my palms are sweating. I can do this. I can separate my personal feelings from my academic pursuits.

William listens intently as I explain my ideas. We don't have to focus on Ophelia's madness, of course. I already know that Tyler's planning an analysis of the sexual undertones of Hamlet's affection for his best friend, Horatio. I'm inspired by Professor Thorne's question about Ophelia's madness, about connecting it to new research on complex PTSD.

He listens intently, his whiskey-colored eyes never leaving mine.

It's unnerving, and enervating, but I push through.

"We see evidence of dissociation, isolation, depression, rage, impulsivity—even aggressiveness. Her death, which has often been attributed to suicide, could be part of the C-PTSD. But it also could be caused by other documented symptoms, including dizziness, chronic fatigue, and even tinnitus."

"Interesting." He considers my words, really mulling them over, which I find more gratifying than I should. "How did you learn so much about C-PTSD?"

My lips turn numb, which is also a symptom.

I am the way I learned so much about it.

The campus health center lets you see a therapist once a month, though it's often randomly assigned. Seeing a new person and starting over each time is exhausting on its own. But one of them mentioned the term to me, and I looked it up.

More people know about PTSD, which is centered around a specific event or series of events. Which means it also has specific triggers. It was understood and described long before it actually made it into the *Diagnostic and Statistical Manual of Mental Disorders.*

Whereas C-PTSD is caused by long-term abuse or neglect, often in childhood. The symptoms are far more wide-ranging—and less understood.

"Complex PSTD is newer," I say, answering his question without really answering it. "Which means it's less likely to have been covered in other papers. There's a lot of important research coming out now that I believe will give us new tools for analyzing Ophelia's characters."

He studies me, as if he's looking right through my careful words, as if he's looking right through *me* to the person who feels permanently damaged, fundamentally different from everyone else, who struggles to form friendships. Knowing those things come from C-PTSD helps me understand, but it doesn't actually make them go away.

It's like I'm made of soggy notepaper, thin and translucent.

He'd tear through me with a single touch of his pen.

Instead, he grabs a book and searches through the pages. "*She stammers, gets upset, takes offense easily...* Gertrude says this about her. What if that's emotional lability?"

My eyebrows rise. It's clear he knows about C-PTSD already.

I step closer, immersing myself in the beauty of words. As we discuss the text, I can feel the tension between us, a constant hum beneath our conversation. It's distracting, but I can't deny that it's also exhilarating.

Somehow I find myself leaning closer, my shoulder brushing against his. His breath catches, and I know he feels it too. It's a dangerous game we're playing.

We continue like this, our voices low, our bodies close. It's a dance, a dance of academia and attraction. And I'm not sure which one is winning.

A loud beep echoes through the library, breaking the spell. The broadcast system announced that the library will be closing soon. Time passed quickly. I have to admit that he's wildly insightful. Compelling. Smart. And this was the most fun I've had…maybe ever.

Stratford glances at his watch. "I had no idea it was so late."

"Thank you for your help. Seriously."

I have pages of notes that I'll work on putting together, formalizing them into a coherent draft that we can then strengthen and revise.

"You're welcome," he says, turning towards me. It's then that I realize I'm only inches away from him. I'm looking at his mouth. And when I glance up, he's looking at mine. "Though I can think of something you can do to repay me."

I can't believe I'm back in this position with Professor Stratford, but my body betrays me with a flash of heat. The public place should provide some shield, but we're tucked away in a secluded corner, the stacks form a private alcove. The rational part of my brain is screaming at me to run as fast as I can.

The heat inside me is louder, more insistent.

"You're supposed to be mentoring me."

The curve of his lips is pure sex. "I love mentoring you."

"This isn't happening."

My heart pounds in my chest as he corners me against the bookshelves, the scent of old leather and ink enveloping us. His words are like a lash, each one stinging more than the last. "I told you what would happen next time I was in the same room with you," he says, his voice low and husky. "I warned you."

My breath hitches as he leans in closer, his eyes dark with desire. "I don't want this," I say, but no one believes me. Not him, not me, not even the books.

"You don't?" he murmurs, his gaze dropping to my lips. "Your body tells a different story. I think it's been hoping for this. You would have gotten a new mentor or done without one if you didn't want this. You wouldn't still be here."

"You're delusional."

"You've touched yourself thinking of me, haven't you? I bet it's the only way you can come, imagining me in your tiny little bed."

I want to deny it, to push him away and storm out of here with my dignity intact.

But ever since that night, he's invaded my thoughts. Even in Hathaway's communal showers, with the steam rising around me, it's his hands I imagined on my skin, his voice whispering filthy things in my ear.

"Go to hell."

A soft, taunting laugh. "Dear Anne."

My heartbeat pounds. *Dear Ophelia.* That's what Claudius said to her after hearing some of her wild thoughts. *How long has she been like this?*

Too long, wanting, needing. Forever.

He presses me against the bookshelves, uneven book spines pressing against my back. Books I might have held or read or cherished now made the witnesses to my debasement. His hand slips into my jeans, his fingers tracing the line of my panties before dipping beneath the fabric.

I gasp, my body arching into his touch instinctively. The sensation of his hand on me, the thrill of doing something so forbidden in such a public place, sends a jolt of arousal coursing through me.

His lips find mine, kissing me with a hunger that matches my own. I surrender to the moment, letting him claim my mouth, my body. His fingers work their magic, stroking and teasing until I'm clinging to him, my moans muffled by his kiss.

His fingers are deft, skilled in a way that makes it impossible to deny the effect he has on me. He's whispering in my ear, his words a mix of Shakespearean prose and filthy promises. I'm caught between the academic part of me that respects him as a mentor and the primal part of me that craves his touch.

Tension coils tighter and tighter, each stroke of his fingers pushing me closer to the edge. He knows exactly what he's doing, how to draw out my pleasure until I'm vibrating with need. I'm trying to stay quiet, to not draw attention to us, but it's a losing battle. Each moan that escapes my lips is a testament to his control over my body.

He watches my face, his eyes alight. "*Sadness, illness, suffering, even Hell itself,*" he murmurs, "*she makes them beautiful.*"

I want to argue, to fight back.

I'm not Ophelia. No. Not mad. Not destined to die.

He's relentless, his fingers moving with a rhythm that leaves me no choice but to surrender to the waves of terrible pleasure crashing over me, trying to drown me.

Orgasm rips through me, breath-taking and soul-stealing, leaving me panting in its wake. I'm clutching at his shoulders, my nails digging into the warm fabric of his shirt, the hard muscles beneath them as I shatter.

As I come down from the high, the reality of the situation starts to sink in. What have I done? I've let myself get swept up in the moment, in the intoxicating mix of dazzling intellect and illicit desire that is Professor William Stratford. I know I should feel ashamed, but all I can seem to muster is a forbidden sense of satisfaction.

"This isn't right," I say, my voice hoarse from sounds I never should have made in a library of all places.

"You can't tell me you didn't want that," he says, a stern expression on his face, the handsome angles made unforgiving by lust. I'm acutely aware that this is the third time he's made me come without any relief for himself.

Yes, I wanted it. The evidence is the way my body still trembles from the aftershocks of my orgasm. And the worst part? I want more. *Push me away if you want to save yourself, because the next time I see you, I'm fucking that beautiful mouth.* I want to remind him what he said, want him to push himself inside me, selfish and crude.

I can't meet his gaze, too embarrassed. "It can't happen again."

"Of course not," he says, though he doesn't believe that. And if I'm being honest, neither do I. "Now, head back to your dorm before they come upstairs to sweep for any lingering students getting finger-fucked behind the stacks."

The harsh words are enough to straighten my back. It's pride that has me shove my books into my bag and toss it over my shoulder without a backward glance. But even as I leave, her song is stuck in my head…

A maid came to his window
To be his Valentine.
He got up, put on his clothes,
And opened the bedroom door,
He let in the maid, but she wasn't a maid
When she departed.

CHAPTER EIGHT

Silence is Golden

As I step out of the library, the cool night air does nothing to clear the fog of lust that still clouds my judgment. My body hums with the remnants of pleasure Stratford's skilled fingers coaxed from me, but I shake my head, trying to dispel the haze.

I'm determined to prove to him, and more importantly, to myself, that I am immune to his charm. That I won't be another notch on his academic belt, a student seduced by her professor's intellect and allure. I square my shoulders and start the brisk walk back to the bar near campus where a lot of people hang out, each step a silent affirmation of my resolve.

Do I like pool and beer?

No, but I'm going to pretend like hell.

As I head down the street, my determined stride falters. There, leaning casually outside the bar, is Brandon. His blond hair catches the moonlight.

He's the epitome of a college heartthrob, with his striking blond hair and a casual ease that seems to draw people in. His brown eyes, paler than his father's, and far less intense, hold a spark of harmless mischief.

He's not handsome the way his father is... But he's cute.

And more importantly, not overwhelming. I'd never lose myself in him. He's young, carefree, and at this moment, what I want to be.

"Hey, Anne," he calls out, pushing off the wall and approaching me. "How was Christmas break? You get any good presents?"

We haven't done presents in our family for a long time. "Sure."

"How's Daisy?"

The genuine concern in his voice surprises me. It's sweet, really, that he's asking about her, though I'm not even sure how she's doing. "She's...coping."

He nods, his brown eyes studying me a moment too long. "That's good. You want to hang out for a bit? It's been a while since we talked."

Since we broke up, he means.

Though somehow my rancor is gone.

We were good together once, even if it was shallow and meaningless and going nowhere. Isn't that what college boyfriends are supposed to be? Even after he cheated, even after I slept with his father, I can't deny the casual comfort his familiar presence brings. It was why I went out with him in the first place.

"Sure, why not," I find myself saying. "I could drink a beer."

He grins, the same charming smile that's a water imitation of his father's. I allow myself to bask in the simplicity of his company. Maybe spending time with him is exactly what I need to remind myself that I'm a 19-year-old college student, not a clandestine lover in a forbidden affair.

I can't help but wonder if Professor Stratford will find out about this.

And if I'm being honest, part of me wants him to.

The Brickside Tavern teems with students. The scent of stale beer welcomes us. Balls click together in rapid succession from the pool tables. He finds us an open one near the back, the green felt worn from countless games. Soon enough we both have beers and sticks, all the accoutrements that should be normal to me. Instead, they feel foreign.

The clack of balls colliding, the whoops of victory, and the indistinct murmur of conversation… It's all strange. I don't usually like this, but it feels so much safer after what Stratford and I did in that library.

Brandon lines up and then breaks the rack. The balls go spinning crazily, two of them landing in the pockets, one of each, which means I get to choose.

"Stripes or solids?" he asks.

"Umm, stripes." I've played pool before. In fact, he's the one who taught me how. Though I'm terrible at it, especially compared to him and his experienced friends. Which is proven when I shoot and the cue ball barely glances off the fifteen.

He hands over one of the little cubes of chalk, which I assume means I should use it on the tip. "How have you been?" he asks.

I've gotten fingered by your father. Twice. "Pretty good. You?"

"I finally transferred to the business department."

"Oh, that's great." I know from when we were dating that he has wanted this for a while. Since before he came to college, actually. "Your mom's cool with it now?"

"No, she still hates it, but my dad actually supports me."

My cheeks burn. "He does?"

"Yeah, we've gotten closer since he started teaching here. He always backed whatever she said, but this time he didn't. Said it was my life, I should get to choose."

I tell him that's great. And it is, because he's never cared about literature, especially the more obscure, unreadable versions of it. He was a year ahead of me. "I never understood why your mother wanted you to study Shakespeare. Sometimes I would envy you."

He snorts. "She wants me to be just like my dad. Which is fucking ironic, because they can't stand each other. They sat on opposite sides of the school auditorium for my high school graduation. Been like that for as long as I can remember."

I shouldn't be pleased that Professor Stratford isn't close to his ex, that he hasn't been for a long time. It shouldn't matter at all, so I ignore the spark of possessiveness.

As the night progresses, Brandon's friends trickle in, a boisterous group that seems to fill the entire bar with their laughter and antics. They're a blur of college stereotypes—baseball caps, fraternity letters, and easy smiles. I watch them, amused by their camaraderie, wincing at some of the immature jokes and the huge bets they place. I'm pressed against the wall, letting others play.

Even when I'm in the middle of the action, I'm outside.

Always on the outside, looking in.

I came here for refuge, but I don't belong here.

The sad truth is that I belong in the library, even if it means being Stratford's lover. Even if it means losing myself in the stacks.

As I watch him, so carefree and unburdened, I can't help but feel a pang of longing for another time. Another life. I was never that way, not even in childhood.

There were no presents wrapped by Santa, only harsh parents who demanded that I love them, love them, love them, until I was a husk of a child. Until I cleaned the house and did the chores and made the money. Until a lifetime spent in fictional plays from the sixteenth century felt more like home.

Brandon catches my eye and grins. He excuses himself from the group and saunters over, a confident swagger in his step. I can't help but smile back, his cheerful tipsiness endearing.

"Having fun?"

"Yeah," I say, trying to prove the point by taking a sip of beer. And wincing.

He laughs. "You never liked that stuff."

I shrug. "It's not my favorite."

Brandon tilts his head, considering me. "What is your favorite?"

Expensive whiskey, as long as it's your father who buys it and teaches me how to drink and watches me as it slides down my throat.

He reaches out, his fingers brushing against mine. I stiffen, surprised by the touch, and pull away slightly. Brandon's smile falters, but he doesn't move his hand. "I know I hurt you. I can't take back what I did, but I miss you."

I bite my lip, my heart pounding in my chest. "I don't know."

He nods, his expression serious. "I understand. But I want you to know that I'm sorry. That if there's any way I could make it up to you, I would."

He leans in, his eyes searching mine, and I know what's coming. I don't move, frozen in place. Part of me wants to try it, to see if maybe, just maybe, kisses like that run in the family. That maybe I could feel that way I did an hour ago against the bookshelf with someone my age.

The other part of me feels, bizarrely, like I'd be cheating.

Professor Stratford has no promises to me. I have none to him. We're not a couple. We're not anything at all, but my skin buzzes with a feeling of *not right*.

His lips meet mine, gentle and hesitant. I close my eyes, my mind filled with the taste of his beer-tinged breath and the sound of the music from the bar. He deepens the kiss, and I try to lose myself, to forget about William and the twisted game we've been playing. It's impossible.

Instead, I find myself comparing Brandon to William, the impatience and clumsiness of his touch to the skilled, dominating caress of William's fingers.

I pull away, breathless. "I can't," I say, the words burning in my throat.

He looks at me, his eyes full of hurt and confusion. "I really fucked this up, didn't I? I was too stupid to know how special you were. I'm sorry."

It's not about his cheating, not really.

It's about realizing that I'm someone else, trying to make myself fit into the mold of a regular college girlfriend, as if he could make me normal.

I'm not sure where I'm going, but I know I need to leave. I turn, my heart pounding, and push past the crowds of students, heading towards the exit.

The campus is a wildfire blur in the setting sun as I weave my way back to my dorm. The elevator car smells so intensely like wet dog that I look around the small space, as if maybe I'm not seeing one. Maybe I just miss Rusty. He was the only good part of home. I'm so lost in thought that I almost miss the looming figure of Lorelei, our ever-vigilant RA. She's telling someone that they have to clean up their shit or they're going to lose shower privileges.

Which feels like a punishment that will hurt all of us.

I manage to step inside without her spotting me.

Something was slipped under my door, a black envelope.

A shiver of apprehension down my spine. The seal of the Shakespeare Society is embossed at the top, a mocking reminder of the privilege that comes with their recognition.

Esteemed scholars,

You are cordially invited to join us for an event that will bring new meaning to the Bard's words. This is not a party. It's a test of intellect, an underground crucible, a gauntlet where wit and cunning reign supreme.

Remember, silence is golden, and the tongue is a double-edged sword. Reveal not the contents of this invitation, lest you slice yourself open.

Jesus Christ. They're inviting me after nearly costing Daisy her life. My blood boils. How dare they? After what they did to her, how could they think I'd want anything to do with them?

I suppose, technically, I passed their initiation.

They disgust me.

Stratford disgusts me. Or at least, he should.

It ends with a skull-shaped QR code that I assume has information on where to go and when. Maybe another few hoops to jump through to keep it secret. Regardless of the threat at the end, people talk.

The Society thrives on power and manipulation.

Professor Stratford does, too. They can have each other. With trembling hands, I crumple the invitation and toss it into the trash bin. I can't believe I let him touch me. In that magic bubble of Shakespeare, I somehow let my guard down. I let myself forget that he's the enemy—and that he's ruthless.

CHAPTER NINE

Dusty, Sacrosanct Air

WINTER FALLS BENEATH a startling and powerful spring, which brings pink flowers to the trees on campus. Coats and sweaters turn to T-shirts and dresses.

I'm busy with Professor Thorne's course. She's a strict taskmaster, but she's not the only thing I have to do. I have Mexican American literature, Sociolinguistics, and a chemistry class to fulfill the single science requirement that I've been putting off.

I cannot care less about oxidation-reduction reactions, unfortunately.

I steel myself against his annoying charm. The last thing I need is a repeat of our last mentorship session. The memory of his touch, the way he commanded my body with such ease, sends a shiver down my spine. I can't—won't—let that happen again. I'm here to win the Tempest Prize.

Nothing more.

As I approach our secluded table, hidden by towering stacks of books, I see him already there, engrossed in a thick volume. His dark hair is tousled, as if he's been running his fingers through it in frustration or deep thought. He looks up as I approach, his deep brown eyes meeting mine with an intensity that momentarily takes my breath away.

"Good afternoon, Ms. Hill." His voice betrays no hint of the intimacy we've shared, and relief mingles with a strange sense of disappointment.

"I've been thinking that in order to show C-PTSD, it needs to appear from the very first scenes where Ophelia appears." I sit down across from him and place my notes-stuffed binder on the table. "Those are the trickiest because she speaks so little, and appears the most docile, but I think I have some leads."

He nods, his gaze scanning the pages I've handed him. His fingers trace the lines of my writing, and I can't help but watch them, remembering their touch. I force myself to focus, to push those thoughts aside.

This is about Shakespeare, about proving myself.

For several minutes, he reads in silence, his

brow furrowed in concentration. I sit across from him, my hands clasped tightly in my lap, waiting for his verdict. Finally, he looks up, his expression serious.

"This is solid."

I try to hide my relief. "Thank you."

"Using the speeches from her father and brother as proof in the absence of her own explanations, the argument that she's been infantilized and insulted, not just in this scene, but all her life. It's compelling."

"They warn her against Hamlet but don't protect her."

"She's responsible for protecting her own virtue," he says, his eyes meeting mine, acknowledgement arcing between us. "Even though she isn't given the tools, she doesn't have the agency against his evil."

My cheeks heat, because I know he's talking about him and me. About what he did to me against the bookshelf. What he might do to me again. I wish my body didn't crave it. I wish I'd been strong enough not to come today.

Though right now he's all business.

He points out specific lines in the scene, suggesting areas for expansion and offering insightful critiques. His feedback is invaluable, challenging me to think more critically about the text and to strengthen my argument. I can't deny his expertise. Or the way he pushes me to be a better scholar.

We fall into a rhythm, discussing themes and character motivations, dissecting each scene with meticulous care. He listens to my ideas, countering with his own interpretations, and together, we explore the depths of Ophelia's mind. It's invigorating, and for a moment, I forget about the tension between us, about the Society and the danger it represents.

As the session comes to a close, Professor Stratford leans back in his chair, his eyes lingering on me. "You have potential, Anne," he says, his voice softer now. "Don't let anyone—including me—distract you from that."

I nod, meeting his gaze with determination. "I won't," I assure him, and for the first time, I actually believe it. "This is my chance to make something of myself, and I'm not going to let anything stand in my way."

Professor Stratford may be a distraction, but he's also a resource, and I plan to use every tool at my disposal to secure my future. Though I sound a bit like Ophelia, reassuring her brother and father that she won't fall victim to Hamlet's many tenders. I can't deny that I feel like her.

I do not know, my lord, what I should think.

"Don't be intimidated by the fact that Professor Thorne is mentoring someone else," he says. "She picks the strongest horse because she wants the prestige that's associated with her student winning. But she's blinded by her ambition. Andini's not the strongest horse. You have something original here. Something powerful."

His confidence in me is intoxicating. "Thank you."

The more time I spend with Professor Stratford, the more I find myself drawn to him. He challenges me, pushes me. Frustrates the hell out of me.

And though I'd never admit it, arouses me.

For sweet-scented moments, I could forget about the Society, *his* Society, that threatens the entire campus. Except they're real. And I can't let myself fall for him. I need to listen to Polonius when he says,

Set your entreatments at a higher rate
Than a command to parle.

"I have to go," I say, shoving my papers into a messy bundle.

"Go where?"

"Hanging out with some friends. Maybe Brandon will be there."

It's a petty move, and I'm rewarded by a flicker of something dark in his eyes. His jaw tightens, and there's a possessive edge to his voice that wasn't there before. "You like him?"

I shrug, feigning nonchalance. "He's a nice guy. Fun to be around."

Professor Stratford leans back in his chair, his eyes never leaving mine. "Brandon is young. He doesn't know what he wants yet."

There's a hint of vulnerability in his words, a subtle admission of his own desire that sends a shiver of pleasure down my spine. As if he's admitting that he wants me. I can't help but feel a secret thrill at his reaction, at the realization that I have the power to affect him just as deeply as he affects me.

The tension between us crackles like static in the air, a palpable force that seems to thicken with every word exchanged. I can see the effect my proximity to his son has on him, and it's intoxicating. It's a dangerous game I'm playing, but the power I hold in this moment is too exhilarating to relinquish. I know this will end badly, but I can't seem to resist.

I've always been a sucker for a good tragedy.

I stand up from my chair, the room suddenly

too hot, too confined.

Professor Stratford stands too, his possessive gaze holds me captive. There's a storm brewing in his deep brown eyes, a tempest that threatens to sweep us both away. "I can't stand the thought of him touching you."

His words send a jolt of electricity straight to my core, igniting a fire that I've been trying desperately to extinguish. I'm playing with fire, and we both know it's only a matter of time before one of us gets burned.

His hand reaches out, fingers gently brushing against my cheek before tangling in my hair. The sensation sends shivers down my spine, and I can feel the warmth between my legs growing more insistent with each passing second.

"Get on your knees," he says.

The demand should outrage me. I should slap him across the face, storm out of the library, and never look back. But I don't. Instead, I find myself obeying, sinking to the floor as the weight of his desire presses down on me.

Hidden by the towering bookshelves, I'm surrounded by the works of Shakespeare—bards and poets, kings and fools—all silent witnesses to our illicit tryst. And as I kneel before him, I can't help but think of the countless scenes of passion and betrayal that have played out within these very walls.

With trembling hands, I reach for his belt, fumbling with the buckle as he watches me with a hunger that borders on desperation. His breath hitches as I free him from his trousers, my fingers wrapping around his hard length.

He's silken steel beneath my touch, hot and pulsing with life. I can feel the rapid beat of his heart through the veins that trace the underside of his cock, a tangible reminder of the power I wield in this moment.

"Lick me. Make me pay for wanting you. Make me beg, dear heart."

The words are like a spell, casting a net of desire that ensnares us both. I part my lips, taking him into my mouth, and the taste of him—salty and slightly bitter—fills my senses. It's a taste that's uniquely his, a flavor that I find myself craving even as my mind rebels against the inevitability of our union.

I move slowly at first, exploring the texture and contours of his manhood with my tongue. His sharp intake of breath is all the encouragement I need to increase my pace, to take him deeper, to revel in the power I hold as he trembles beneath my touch.

His fingers tighten in my hair, guiding me, urging me on as he chases the release that I know

I can give him. And when he finally succumbs, his body shuddering with the force of his orgasm, the sound of his pleasure—a low, guttural moan that echoes through the silent library—is the sweetest song.

As he slumps against the bookshelf, spent and sated, triumph runs through my veins, alongside the simmering arousal. I have part of him that no one else does, claiming my power in a world that always tries to control me.

Every victory comes at a cost.

For every moment of pleasure we share, we are drawn deeper into the dangerous dance of our mutual destruction. And though I may be on my knees now, it is not submission that holds me here—it is the undeniable truth that in this game of hearts and minds, I am just as complicit as he is.

Without a word, he guides me gently to a nearby pile of large, wide tomes, their leather-bound covers well-worn and aged. He gently settles me on top of them, kneeling before me, his hands tracing the curves of my body before settling on my hips. The stack of ancient tomes beneath me feels like a throne, his posture almost like a supplicant.

The smooth leather feels cool beneath my ass. Stratford bends down, his lips brushing against my inner thigh. The anticipation builds inside me, a fire that threatens to consume me whole.

His tongue meets my cunt, and I can't hold back any longer. My hands grip the edges of the ancient pages, the leather-bound books flexing beneath the force of my passion.

"Please." My voice echoes through the silent space, a testament to the eternal desire that courses through me.

"You taste too good. I don't want this to end."

It goes on and on. His tongue is relentless, licking and teasing, pushing me over the edge again and again. The pleasure is almost too much to bear, and yet I crave more, my body responding with an urgency that I've never felt before. I'm helpless to resist, lost in a sea of sensation that I never want to escape.

Stratford brings me to the brink of ecstasy, his touch both tender and demanding. My moans of pleasure fill the dusty, sacrosanct air.

I'm not just losing myself in this moment.

I'm finding myself, too.

These forbidden encounters with Stratford may be reckless, dangerous even, but it has also given me something that I've never had before: a sense of belonging, a connection that transcends the boundaries of lust and love.

CHAPTER TEN

The Skull Scene

THE NEXT CLASS with Professor Thorne begins with the rustle of papers and the crisp scent of books in the air. There's a palpable energy in the room today, a vibrating anticipation that makes my heart beat a little faster. I settle into my seat, my notebook open and ready, my pen poised like a sword ready to duel.

Professor Thorne strides into the room, her presence commanding silence from the chattering students. She sets her materials down on the lectern with a decisive thud, and then, with a dramatic pause that captures everyone's attention, she announces, "I have some exciting news regarding the Tempest Prize."

The room buzzes with interest, and I can't help but lean forward, hanging on her every word. "This year," she continues, "in addition to the prestige, the prize will include guaranteed publication by one of the best peer-reviewed journals on Shakespeare."

Whoa. Publication? My eyes widen, and I feel a surge of excitement. Everyone sits up straighter. Publication as an undergrad is almost unheard of. The prospect of winning isn't just about the prestige anymore; it's about the freedom. I think of my parents, their voices laced with condescension and cruelty, and how this prize could be my ticket to a life free from their grasp, proof that I belong here.

Professor Thorne's gaze sweeps across the room, pausing briefly on each of us as if to gauge our reactions. When her eyes land on Matteo, she gives him a nod of approval, her lips curling into a rare smile. "Matteo is doing exceptional work," she says, her voice carrying through the lecture hall. "I have no doubt he'll be a formidable contender for the Tempest."

The words sting, but I refuse to let them deter me. I glance at Matteo, taking in his designer clothes and the air of privilege that surrounds him.

He doesn't need the money.

Professor Thorne begins the lecture, which is about betrayal and its many representations in the play: Claudius's betrayal of Hamlet's father and

Hamlet himself.

"Ms. Hill," she calls, her tone sharp and commanding.

The entire class turns to look at me, their eyes piercing me with the weight of their expectations. I sit up straighter, my throat tight.

Professor Stratford ran his class in a more casual way, almost like a salon where each person's contributions were valued. In contrast, Thorne runs her classroom as if it's always an oral exam. A student who is called on has only seconds to answer a specific question with a cogent, thoughtful response.

"Hamlet's response to betrayal," she asks, "would you say that it's melodramatic? Or that it's an authentic portrayal?"

What even is an authentic response to betrayal?

Stratford's betrayal is a fresh wound, a sting that hasn't yet dulled.

"Hamlet's actions are often described as being excessive. But perhaps that is Shakespeare's intention. To illustrate the depth of betrayal's impact, to demonstrate how it can drive a person to the brink of insanity."

I pause, my gaze meeting Professor Thorne's. There's a flicker of approval in her eyes, a brief acknowledgment before she nods and swiftly moves on to the next question, the next student. The class resumes its usual rhythm, but I remain stuck on the betrayal. Maybe I'm the one going insane.

The door to the lecture hall creaks open. Tyler stumbles in, his usual cocky grin replaced by a haggard expression. My heart clenches at the sight of him—his eyes are bloodshot, and there's a dullness to them that wasn't there before. He moves slowly, favoring his right side as he limps to his seat.

He's late, something Professor Thorne doesn't tolerate well.

"Mr. Levine," she says, her voice cold with reproval. "How kind of you to grace us with your presence. I do hope whatever kept you from punctuality was more important than your academic career."

"Sorry," he mumbles, his voice hoarse.

Thorne's red lips press together. "Don't let it happen again."

He nods, looking down at his desk, a flush creeping up his neck. Concern for him rises as he keeps his gaze down, not even bothering to pull out paper to take notes. What's wrong with him?

Class resumes, but I can't focus on Thorne's

words anymore. I need to know if Tyler is okay. Ripping a page from my notebook, I quickly scrawl a message. *What's wrong?*

I slide it gently across my desk.

Tyler reads it, glancing at me with an expression that's difficult to decipher. He scrawls something quickly.

I expect something serious or at least playful, the way he usually is. Instead, he's written only a single word, *Nothing.*

It's obviously a lie. Something bad must have happened.

A problem at home? A fight with a friend?

My gaze flits back to Professor Thorne, who's now lecturing on the themes of loyalty and madness in *Hamlet*, of friendship and family, and the way they have the power to hurt us the most. I attempt to focus and take notes, so that maybe I'll be able to catch up later, when my brain can focus on what she's saying.

The class ends, and Tyler moves with surprising quickness despite the stiffness in his gait. I catch up to him, concern pushing aside politeness.

"Hey. What's wrong?"

He turns in the hallway, his face a mask of reluctance. "Leave it."

His words bite, but I'm not one to back down

easily, not when a friend is in trouble. "It seems like you're in pain. Did you get hurt or something?"

His eyes dart back to me, surprise and a hint of fear flickering.

"Oh my God. You *are* hurt. What the hell happened?"

A long, blown-out breath. "It's the Society."

The *Shakespeare* Society. This was my fear. "The gauntlet thing?"

He doesn't shake his head or nod, just looks at me.

Anger tears through me. "What did they do to you?"

"You didn't go, so why do you care?"

I cross my arms, ready to face off with him. "I care because you're my friend. I care about you. Now, what happened?"

Tyler looks away, and I think he won't tell me, but then he sighs. "Fine, but you didn't hear this from me. It was supposed to be a crazy stunt, like just for fun. You know how in *Hamlet*, the skull scene."

"The one with Yorick?"

"Yeah, like that's fucked up. You're hanging out with a gravedigger, and then it turns out you're holding the skull of a guy you knew?"

"It was messed up to be hanging out with a gravedigger regardless, but sure."

He looks at me, his eyes dark with anguish he doesn't want to show. "That was the stunt. Some of us got shovels. And some of us got…buried."

Bile rises in my throat. "What?"

"I knew it was stupid. And dangerous. So blame it on me."

"I'm going to blame it on both of you, but mostly on them."

He gives an uneven laugh. "I thought the whole thing would be a laugh. And maybe there'd be an orgy at the end of it. But all the dirt, the dark. I felt like I was running out of air. I think I might have passed out."

"Christ," I whisper. "You need to go to campus health services."

"And tell them what?"

"How about the truth?"

He snorts, sounding slightly more like himself. "Hardly. I would be implicating myself, since this took place in the south quad. Somehow I don't think they got a permit. Besides, I'm not, like, harmed."

"You don't seem exactly healthy and hale."

"I've got some bruises, but it's mostly the mindfuck of it all."

"So get them in trouble. They deserve it for what happened to you."

Tyler shakes his head. "I knew the risks when I joined. I won't go to one of their things again, but I can't go up against them. They're too powerful."

"They need to be stopped."

"You know, I might finally agree with you."

"They can't just keep getting away with this."

His gaze locks on mine, and for the first time, I see a flicker of desperation. "Whatever you're thinking of doing, Anne, *don't*. No one can stand up to them. They know they can get away with anything. They have too much influence in the university. And they're out of control."

Anger bubbles up inside me, hot and acidic. "We can go tell Dean Morris," I say. "This has gone too far. People could have been killed."

Tyler shakes his head, adamant. "If I snitch, it'll only get worse."

"Worse?" I echo, incredulous. "Tyler, look at you! You're lucky to be walking at all. What if it had been worse? What if next time—"

"There won't be a next time," he cuts me off, his voice firm despite the pain he's obviously in. "I'm out. I'm done with the Society."

My thoughts turn to Professor Stratford, the

man who introduced me to the wonders of Shakespeare, the same man who is deeply entrenched in the Society's dangerous escapades. How can he be a part of something so reckless?

How can he put his students at risk like this?

I feel a sudden surge of betrayal, not just for myself, but for Tyler and every other student who has fallen prey to the Society's allure. I believed that Professor Stratford's interest in me was genuine, but I've been fooling myself all along.

"Please report this. It's not just about you anymore."

"I said no," he replies, his voice pained but resolute. "I shouldn't even have told you that much. Stay away from them. I certainly plan to."

There's a finality in his words that tells me pressing further will only push him away. He walks away, his head down, steps still uneven. His body will heal from the Society's cruel brand of fun. Though it will take his mind much longer.

CHAPTER ELEVEN

Court of Elsinore

MOVIE NIGHT IS a sacred tradition among friends, and after the stress of the past few days, I'm more than ready for some mindless entertainment.

The door swings open, revealing Carlisle's bright smile. "You made it!"

"Wouldn't miss it."

Her suite at the Mayfair dorms is a stark contrast to the cramped boxes we get in Hathaway. It's large and airy, with modern furnishings that somehow still manage to convey a sense of coziness. The aroma of popcorn fills the air, mingling with the scent of melted butter.

It's comforting after worrying about a big, scary, secret society.

Carlisle closes the door behind us and leans against it, her expression turning wistful. "You know, I sometimes forget how nice it is to have a normal evening," she says, her voice tinged with a hint of melancholy.

"They're still after you?" I ask with sympathy.

She makes a face. "Someone stuck a phone into a bathroom stall I was in. Thankfully, I hadn't sat down yet, but…yuck."

"That's horrible."

She shrugs. "It's the life I chose, or at least, the life that chose me. But sometimes, I just want to be a regular college student."

When I first met her at orientation, I didn't know who she was.

Then I learned she was Carlisle Lockwood, the childhood movie star and teen pop singer. I thought we'd never speak again. What could we have in common? Except she wants someone to treat her like a regular college person.

And I've learned that money doesn't solve problems.

Even if a little more would help.

We all have our own battles, our own versions of a life that's both a blessing and a curse. "Well, tonight, you're just Carlisle, my friend and rom-com enthusiast," I say. "So, what'll it be tonight?"

Her face lights up, the shadows of her public persona fading away. "I was thinking we could start with a classic, *How to Lose A Guy in Ten*

Days."

I nod, as if I know what that means. She's been trying to fill in the gaps of my pop culture knowledge. We joke that it's a class I'm taking at Tanglewood University. It could be called Modern Terminology for Chronically Nose-in-a-Book People.

"But then I thought…*Princess Bride?*"

"Is that the one where she finds out she's a long-lost princess?" I vaguely remember people talking about that one in school.

"Umm, no. That's something totally different. You'll like *Princess Bride*. It's got old things in it."

I grin at her description of my tastes. Old things like Shakespeare and Renaissance literature. Oh, and Professor Stratford. I do like him, unfortunately.

"I'm in your capable hands," I say, settling onto the plush sofa, its cushions enveloping me in a warm embrace. Carlisle joins me, her eyes sparkling as she queues up the movie. She plays it from her phone, casting it into a huge flat screen that's set into a picture frame.

As the opening credits roll, I find myself momentarily transported away from the drama of the Shakespeare Society, the haunting image of Tyler's injured form, and the complicated feelings

I harbor for Professor Stratford.

We laugh together at the comedic antics of the Dread Pirate Roberts and Vizzini, of the lasting love between Buttercup and Westley.

Inigo Montoya has finally found the man who killed his father—Prepare to die—when an alert pops up on the screen.

New mention, it says. By Tanglewood Tea.

It shows the opening line. "The Shakespeare Society brings drama, literally. Meanwhile, Carlisle Lockwood …"

The text cuts off.

"What are they saying about you now?"

The anonymous campus gossip site doesn't often talk about her, probably because she's gotten so good at hiding in her dorm room. And watching out for jerks in bathrooms. But when they do mention her, it's never complimentary.

Her cheeks have turned pink, betraying her emotion even as she tells me, "It doesn't matter."

I'm already on my phone.

Meanwhile, Carlisle Lockwood once again thinks that she's the only person on campus who can sing. A reliable source says she'll be singing the national anthem at the spring football game. Maybe after that she can stop throwing herself so desperately at the media.

"You didn't tell me you were singing at the football game."

"For one thing, you don't care about football."

"Yeah, but I'd go to support you."

"Tickets sold out a long time ago. I could probably get you in… But I wouldn't subject you to that."

"I mean, I wouldn't want to watch the ball stuff."

She grins and then sobers. "They're just doing it for the ratings boost. I'm not the best singer here, obviously."

"You're a great singer, and I hate that they get to make you feel bad."

"Nah, it's just the truth. The music department here is world class. I would have said no so they could pick someone else, but then people would have said I was being stuck up, thinking I'm too good to participate in my own college."

"You should sue them. They can't just write anything they want about you and get away with it."

She looks at me with a mixture of amusement and resignation. "That's how it works, actually. The tabloids, the online socials. My lawyers told me a long time ago to ignore it, that going after them isn't worth it."

"It's still not right."

"Besides," she says, "the people behind Tanglewood Tea are anonymous. There's no one to sue. And don't suggest subpoenaing the social sites. That never works. They're locked down tighter than the freaking Pentagon."

"How can they get away with lying?"

"Maybe it's not a lie. Maybe I am desperate for media coverage."

I snort. "You wouldn't be in here hanging out with a rando like me if you cared about being seen in the media."

"You're not a rando. You're my friend."

I can't help myself. I look down to read the rest of the post, this time aloud for Carlisle's benefit.

The Shakespeare Society has reached the next act of their super exclusive, goth emo, asshole elitism play. There wasn't much dancing or public sex at their last event. In fact, we aren't clear on the specifics of what did happen, but we do know that three students ended up in the hospital, with one dropping out of TU for the semester in favor of a mental hospital. Rumor has it the Society isn't planning to drop the curtain anytime soon.

I rub my forehead where worry has formed a knot.

Carlisle also looks concerned, but it's focused on me. "They sound pretty scary. You're not still going to their stuff, are you?"

I shake my head. "No, I gave my invitation to this stunt to someone at the school who's trying to shut them down. But apparently he couldn't stop it."

"Maybe he's part of it."

My cheeks flush. I never told her about Professor Stratford. "I don't think so. He's ex-military. Super honorable."

"Maybe, but professors are involved. Parents, too."

"What?"

"That's the only reason it's still happening."

"There's this guy in some of my classes. Tyler. He went. It really messed him up."

Her eyes widen. "Is he okay?"

"He will be, but it was bad," I explain, the memory of Tyler's battered form still fresh in my mind. "It seems like they're escalating."

"Look, I really don't want you to get hurt. And getting mixed up with them is probably a terrible idea, but…"

When she doesn't finish the thought, I say,

"I'm already mixed up with them. You know what happened to Daisy."

"Is she doing okay?"

I still didn't know how to answer that. She's not in a mental hospital. But then, maybe she should be. I don't think pretending like nothing is wrong is helping.

"I don't know," I say, opting for honesty.

"I can't believe I'm even going to say this, but maybe you should go to the next event. You could use your invite to go undercover, so to speak. Gather evidence, expose them for what they really are."

It could help put a stop to their dangerous games.

Or it could land me in the mental health hospital, too.

"I want to help, to fight back, but I'm not exactly a James Bond."

She reaches out, her hand covering mine in a reassuring gesture. "You're strong and brave and smart. So, does Bond have some gadgets? Sure, but... Wait, don't tell me you haven't watched one yet."

"It doesn't matter. The dean specifically asked me to stay away from the Society. He says it's too dangerous, and after seeing this, I think he's right."

"No, of course he is. It was just a crazy idea. Forget I said anything."

"I need to keep my grades up for my scholarship, and with how much time I've spent on that prize I mentioned, it hasn't been easy."

"Yes, totally. School is the most important thing."

"Why does it feel like you're just saying that?"

"You're completely right. It *is* too dangerous. And you *should* focus on school. It's just… If not you, then who? You're one of the few people who has both the courage and the access to do something about it. The Society is out of control, and someone needs to expose them before more people get hurt."

"I'll think about it."

Her words resonate with me, stirring a sense of responsibility. I'm torn between my own survival instinct and the undeniable pull of justice. I think of Tyler, his face pale with pain, and the fear in Dean Morris's eyes when he spoke of the Society's escalating antics.

The conversation moves on to Carlisle's life, in which her mother continues being a problem. She wants her to go back to performing concerts and starring in Netflix movies. She claims she's worried about Carlisle's career taking a hit that she'll regret later. But Carlisle thinks she just wants the cut she gets as her manager.

Ironically, this is something we have in common. Whether it's a few hundred dollars or a few million, neither of our parents mind exploiting us.

It's late by the time I leave, stepping out of her room into the hallway.

I'm so lost in my thoughts that I almost stumble upon them—Matteo, locked in a passionate embrace with another man. Unlike the Hathaway, this dorm doesn't split up genders, so it's not weird to find guys here. Though it is a little awkward to see a classmate I barely know in such an intimate position.

I move to squeeze by them, but Matteo looks up, locking eyes with me. His expression shifts from surprise to anger, and I feel a jolt of animosity.

"Anne Hill," he says with disdain. "Out for a late-night stroll?"

"I was just hanging out with someone. No biggie." I try to make it clear I have no problem with him and whatever he's doing before walking away, but he follows me, leaving his partner in the shadows.

"I know whose room that is. Carlisle Lockwood, pop star, cokehead, slut—"

"Shut the hell up."

He grins. "Or maybe you were only waiting until I was around, stalking me for something intelligent to say about *Hamlet*."

"Wow, the ego on you needs its own zip code."

I walk away when he adds, "You know, you could spend all the time in the world with that mentor of yours, and it still wouldn't get you close to winning the Tempest Prize."

His words hit me like a slap, and my resolve crumbles. "What's that supposed to mean?" I demand, my voice trembling with anger.

Matteo laughs, the sound grating in the stillness of the night. "You're out of your league here. There's zero chance of beating me, no matter how hard you try. So forget about the Tempest Prize."

I bristle at his words. "I guess we'll see."

"May the best man win. That's me, by the way."

I know he's just trying to get under my skin, to shake my confidence, but I'm afraid he might be right. I walk the rest of the way back to my dorm lost in thought, Matteo's derisive laughter ringing in my ears.

The elevators in Hathaway are broken.

Again.

I trudge up three flights of stairs to my dorm room, the weight of the day pressing down on me. The encounter with Matteo has left a bitter taste in my mouth. I push open the door, grateful for the sanctuary of my small, cluttered room. The Hathaway is old and smelly, but it's where I belong—unlike the glittering, cutthroat glamor of Mayfair.

Daisy is asleep, her chest rising and falling in a peaceful rhythm, her blonde hair splayed out on the pillow. She looks so serene, so untouched by the pain. I hope it leaves her alone in her dreams at least.

As I change into my pajamas, my eyes catch a glimpse of something on my desk—a thick envelope, embossed with the seal of the Shakespeare Society. My heart skips a beat. I know what it is without even opening it. Another invitation.

I approach the desk with caution, as if the envelope might explode at any moment.

I look back at my roommate, her features softened by sleep. She survived but at what cost? And Tyler still doesn't look the same. How many more will suffer before someone puts a stop to it?

A fierce determination takes hold of me. I can't stand by and do nothing while my friends get hurt. It's time to take a stand.

And as Carlisle said, if not me, then who?

I open the envelope and read the elegant script.

For some reason, this one has my name.

Ms. Hill,

You are invited to join the court of Elsinore, where madness and reason wage war, where life and death face off in a timeless battle. This event is not for the faint of heart. Come if you dare…but know that your attendance means complete and utter surrender.

God, they're dramatic.

What kind of bullshit thing are they going to do this time? An underground party with themed cocktails and gambling and even an orgy was fun enough. Risky enough. It's clear they're getting worse. Getting more intense. Getting more dangerous.

The gravedigger stunt? Insane.

And this invitation sounds worse than the last.

Then again, if I'm too afraid to face the real world, with all its shadows, then I might as well go home. Might as well move back in with my parents and support them and their delusions until I die.

My survival instincts tell me to stay away from Stratford. Another voice whispers in the back of my mind, insidious and compelling. What if I'm the only one who can get close enough to uncover the truth? What if, by some twist of fate, I'm the key to stopping him?

The vow comes to me with the moonlight casting long shadows across the room. I'll attend the Society's next gathering. And I will do whatever it takes to bring the Shakespeare Society down, to expose them for the danger they are.

For Daisy.

For Tyler.

For the university.

For myself.

And maybe, somehow, even for Professor Stratford. It's time he understood the true cost of his twisted extracurricular activities. He has to be stopped. It might as well be by someone who's been foolish enough to fall for him.

CHAPTER TWELVE

A Promising Future

DEAN BLAKE MORRIS, the gold placard reads.

The door, solid oak, feels like a barrier between me and a path to redemption. My knuckles rap against the wood, the sound sharp and final in the quiet hallway.

"Come in," a voice calls from within, and I push the door open, stepping into the room. Dean Morris looks up from his desk, his face a mask of stern professionalism that softens slightly as our eyes meet. "Anne," he says, his voice a deep rumble, "it's good to see you. Please, have a seat."

I settle into the chair opposite him, my fingers gripping the armrests. The room is impeccably neat, shelves lined with books on military history and framed photographs.

"Looks like something's on your mind," he says, leaning back in his chair, his scarred hands folded on the desk. There's a kindness in his eyes that makes me want to spill my guts, to unburden myself of the tangled mess.

I take a deep breath, the words I've been rehearsing for days finally finding their way out. "Last semester you asked me to let you know about the Shakespeare Society. I got this last night."

I hand him the torn pieces of the invitation, which is still a bit crumpled from when I took it out of the trash. It feels like a betrayal of Professor Stratford to share this. Worse even than kissing Brandon. But I have to choose my side, and it's going to be Tanglewood University. It's going to be my friends, not some twisted affair.

He studies it. "Thank you for showing me."

"I also need to tell you something. Something that's hard to say."

He nods, his expression encouraging me to continue. "Go ahead."

"It's about Professor Stratford," I say, the name tasting like dark spices on my tongue. "I believe he's involved with the Shakespeare Society."

His eyebrows shoot up, but he doesn't interrupt me.

"I found some stuff that shows he was part of the Society back when he was a student. And I know some students got expelled last semester, but that didn't stop them." I can't admit that I overheard him talking to Stratford about the society, because then I'd also admit to skulking around the Provost's house. "They're still here."

"I understand your concerns. Professor Stratford was in the Society during his time here as a student, but he's an adult now. A professor. He's working to protect the students, not harm them. The Society is dangerous. He wants to stop them."

"I believe he came back to help them. That's why he accepted the job."

The dean's gaze meets mine with an unsettling directness. "I can see why you might think that, but I trust him."

Frustration flickers through me. "What if you're wrong?"

He sighs. "I was wrong to ask you to be my informant. It puts you at risk. It put Ms. Bradshaw at risk. I don't want you to look into them anymore. If they send you another one of these invitations, throw it away."

"What?"

"They're escalating, which means it's more dangerous now than ever."

The seriousness in his voice is a stark reminder

of the stakes. Fear shivers through me. Part of me is relieved by his words. I've been dancing on the edge of a precipice, drawn to the Society's allure and repelled by its danger.

Walking away tempts me.

Except I can't just forget what I've seen, what I've experienced.

My gaze lands on the photograph on his desk, a beautiful woman with dark hair holding a child—his family. There's an ache in my chest, an envy for the obvious love in that image, the pure joy on his child's face. Next to the photo, another frame holds artwork made from fingerpaint and uncooked pasta.

It strikes a chord deep within me.

Family can be so sweet. Sometimes.

My own family doesn't have photos like that.

Dean Morris follows my line of sight. His features soften into a quiet reverence when he sees her picture. Despite the rough terrain of the scar, he looks tender, the look of a man whose foundation lies with those precious faces.

His voice is husky. "Erin was a student here. Please believe me that I would never allow anyone of you to be hurt if I could help it. I'm doing everything I can to root out the Society for good."

I hear the honesty in his voice. He believes

what he's saying, and why shouldn't he? The medals, the scar—he's a protector. A man of honor.

That doesn't mean he's right about Professor Stratford.

"I can't just ignore this," I say. "Daisy is my best friend. If something were to happen, if someone gets hurt, and I did nothing…"

He holds up a hand, stopping me mid-sentence. "I understand your concern, but it's not safe. You're a bright young woman with a promising future. I won't have you putting yourself in harm's way for this."

I feel the sting of disappointment. It's not just about the Society anymore. It's about trust—about the man who has become both my mentor and my tormentor. Stratford's pull on me is magnetic, and I know that as long as he's involved, I'll be drawn back into the fray, no matter the risks.

"I'll handle this from here, Ms. Hill. Focus on your studies. That's where your future lies. Now, is there anything else you need to tell me?"

There's a battle inside me. What would Dean Morris say if I told him what Professor Stratford did to me in the library? What he did to me in the dorm room? It would probably be enough to drive him away from the school, regardless of whether he's part of the Society or not.

Except I can't bring myself to say the words out loud.

What happened between us is too secret. Too sacred.

And I'm an idiot.

What we have isn't sacred, but it still feels unfair to tell on him. He's never coerced me. And he's protected me in his own way, like at the Pinnacle.

"No, sir."

The dean seems disappointed, but he accepts it with a nod.

I leave the office a whirl of emotions. Relief, because I've shared my burden with someone who has the power to act. Worry, because the stakes are higher than I'd imagined. And anger—so much anger, because Stratford continues to pull my strings.

They're escalating, which means it's more dangerous now than ever.

What exactly does that mean? The Society's antics have always been on the fringe of acceptability, but this seems worse. And Stratford is at the center of it all. He's clever, charismatic, and manipulative—the perfect storm for the Society's dark plans.

Part of me rebels against the idea. Part of me wants to believe the dean is right about him, even though I was there the night I saw the tattoo, the night I found those boxes of Society paraphernalia, the night he told me to get the hell out.

That's the terrible beauty of William Stratford.

Even knowing what he is, I don't really want to escape.

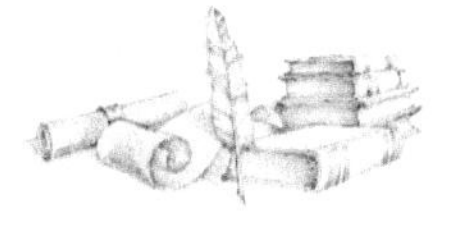

CHAPTER THIRTEEN

Punishment

AT THE THIRD mentor session, Professor Stratford glances up, his eyes skimming over the stack of binders in my arms before settling on my face. A single dark eyebrow arches upward in that infuriating and incredibly sexy way of his.

"You've been busy," he says.

"We found out about the whole journal thing. That the winner will get published." The words tumble out in a rush, my excitement momentarily overriding the tension that always seems to simmer between us.

Stratford leans back in his chair. "I wondered if you'd have time between dating Brandon. Or if you'd even care about publication."

Wow. I set the stack down on the table with a thud. I'm determined to ignore the comment about Brandon, but it stings. "I've been going through every academic journal I could find, every critique, every analysis…anything that could give me an edge."

"Let's see what you've got."

As I take my seat across from him, I can't help but feel a twinge of apprehension. He seems sharper today, harder. Meaner. I push the feeling aside, reminding myself of the progress I've made, of the late nights and the countless hours spent poring over Shakespeare's texts.

Stratford sifts through the pages, his eyes scanning the lines of text, the marginal notes, the highlighted passages. Every so often, he pauses, his brow furrowing in concentration or lifting in surprise. I study his reactions, eager for any sign of approval, any hint that I'm on the right track.

"That publication you'd win? It doesn't only have your name on it. It has the name of your mentor. Thorne might not have mentioned that."

Shit. Our names would be together, etched into the same place. Years from now, decades, if that paper is ever cited, it will have both our names. In my own listings of publications and CV, it would have his name.

That is disturbing.

What's most disturbing is the small swell of pleasure it gives me.

I frown at the last sentence. "Are you saying

that's why she pushes this prize? Why she does the whole best-student-gets-mentored thing?"

"Why else?"

"She already has publications."

"More is more when you want to be the best Shakespeare scholar."

I glare at him. Professor Thorne is not my favorite person, but I'm not going to talk shit about her with him on the basis of gender. "And you somehow *don't* want credit for your work?"

"Of course I do. I was warning you, in case you want to switch mentors."

My eyes widen. He's already done a bunch of work. Even if I did switch mentors for some reason, he'd deserve credit. "I don't care who else is on there. My name being on a publication would be a huge deal."

He mutters something under his breath.

"What?"

"I said you deserve to be published."

My heart leaps at his words. "Thank you," I say, trying to keep my voice even, to not betray how much his praise matters to me.

He leans forward, his eyes locked on to mine. "You deserve it," he says, his tone serious, "but shit like this is not just about deserving. There are a million things that factor into a prize like this.

Who's won before, how the argument lands with the judges. Even who knows who."

"Who knows who?"

"The world isn't fair. You know that. It's why you have to find some old fucker at a hotel bar to buy your textbooks."

"You aren't that old."

He meant Grandpa, but I like being the one to tease him. His lips quirk, and for a moment, the rest of the world fades away. The prize, the Society. It's just the two of us, bound by secrets and lies and a shared love of Shakespeare.

Then he frowns, as if he caught himself, as if enjoying himself is forbidden. "Get it all together, the outline, the references," he says. "Tonight. I want the first draft in my inbox tomorrow for review."

I start gathering up the sheets, thrown off by his cold tone. "I can't work on it tonight but I'll have time on Sunday."

"It's Friday night. What else do you have to do tomorrow?"

I cross my arms, torn between laughter and annoyance. "This might shock you, but I do have a social life. Not a big one, but it exists."

"So you care more about fucking some frat boy than Shakespeare?"

Annoyance wins. "No, but even if I did, that's not your business."

"It is if I'm the one mentoring you, spending time on you. Why am I doing that if you don't even give a shit about the Tempest Prize?"

My whole body flushes hot.

It moves through me fast, too fast, leaving me seasick and clammy. The last time we met, things had been different. He was warm, even playful.

Now he seems determined to be an asshole.

"I care about the prize—about the prestige. About the money. About the analysis, even." I take a deep breath, trying to ignore the hurt of his accusations. "But I won't be working on the draft tonight. I have plans, and I won't break them just because you snap at me."

His eyes narrow. "What are you doing tonight?"

"Hanging out?"

"With a bunch of dumb kids?"

I glare at Professor Stratford, my heart pounding with a mix of anger and defiance. "Dumb kids like your son?" I challenge, my voice rising in the silent library. The words taste bitter on my tongue, but I won't back down. I've had enough of his condescension, his arrogance.

A small smile curves his lips. "I know you

aren't fucking Brandon."

"Fine," I retort, my hands balled into fists at my sides. "Maybe I'm seeing someone else." It's a lie, but I relish the flash of jealousy that crosses his face.

His eyes narrow, and I can see the gears turning in his mind. Unfortunately for me, he's smart—even if he is a jerk. "It's not a date at all, is it?" he says, his voice low and dangerous. "You're going to the Society event."

I lift my chin defiantly, meeting his gaze with my own. "So what if I am?" I say, my voice steady despite the pounding of my heart. I won't let him intimidate me, won't let him control me.

"Absolutely not," he snaps, his eyes flashing with anger.

I snort, unable to contain my frustration. "I didn't ask for your permission."

I'm tired of being told what to do, tired of being treated like a child.

His face hardens, and for a moment, he looks every inch the formidable professor that he is. Every inch the sinister leader of the Shakespeare Society.

"I forbid it," he says.

"Excuse me?" My voice rises in disbelief. "You don't get to forbid me anything, Professor

Stratford. I'm not your student, your daughter, or your girlfriend. I'm nothing to you."

"You're the little girl wandering around the forest. I'm the wolf. I know you spoke to the dean. It won't fucking work. You think you can take me down? I can ruin you with a few words, destroy any chance of you winning the Tempest Prize. Or having a career in this field at all. So stay the fuck away from the event."

"If you didn't want me to go, then why send me an invite?" His expression tightens, a flicker of something—worry, perhaps—crossing his features. "Oh, I see," I continue, a bitter edge to my words. "You don't completely control them, do you? Not completely. Which means you can't stop me from attending."

He steps towards me, his eyes dark and intense. "Anne," he warns, his voice low and dangerous, "if you attend that event, there will be consequences."

I raise an eyebrow, refusing to be intimidated. "Consequences?" I repeat, my tone mocking. "What are you going to do, fail me? Oh wait, I'm not in your class."

He moves closer, heat radiating off his large body. "I'll spank you."

For a moment, I'm too stunned to speak.

The idea is so absurd, so unexpected, that I can't help but laugh. The sound dies in my throat when I realize he's serious. "You wouldn't dare," I whisper, my heart pounding in my chest.

He leans in, his lips brushing against my ear. "Oh, I would," he murmurs, his voice filled with dark promise. "I'd bend you over my knee, lift that pretty skirt of yours, and spank you until your ass turns a beautiful red."

A flush of heat floods through me, and I can feel my cheeks burning with a mix of embarrassment and arousal. I'm shocked by my own reaction, by the way my body responds to his words. I've always known that there's a thin line between pleasure and pain, but I never imagined that I'd be standing on that precipice with Professor Stratford.

"Yes," he murmurs, his large fingers brushing my flushed cheeks. "That color. I'll enjoy it. After I've spanked the rebellion out of you, you'll enjoy it, too."

I step back, putting some much-needed distance between us. "Never."

His gaze rakes over me with an intensity that sends shivers down my spine. "You don't want to challenge me in this, Anne. I'll win."

I'm spooked by my own desires, by the realization that a part of me wants to experience the dark thrill of his punishment. But I won't give in to that temptation, won't let him have that power over me.

Besides, that event is not about a good time.

It's about avenging Daisy and Tyler. About protecting the school.

"I'm going. There's nothing you can do to stop me. Even if you spanked me, I'd still go, but you aren't going to do that."

"Is that so?" he murmurs, stepping towards me with a dangerous grace. I can feel the heat of his body, the magnetic pull of his presence.

I have to call his bluff. We're in the freaking library, for Christ's sake.

His hands grip my waist and lift me off the ground as if I weigh nothing. I gasp, my heart racing as he maneuvers me onto the study table, its surface littered with books and papers. His strength is both terrifying and thrilling, and a part of me can't help but respond to his dominance.

With a swift motion, he bends me over the desk, my cheek pressed against the cool wood. I can feel the fabric of my skirt being lifted, his hands skimming over the curves of my ass with a possessive intent.

"Did you wear this skirt for me?" he growls,

his voice thick with desire. "Did you want me to see your ass, to imagine all the wicked things I could do to it?"

I squirm, my face flushing with a mixture of embarrassment and arousal. "I didn't—" I start to protest, but he cuts me off with a sharp smack to my backside. The sound reverberates through the quiet library, and I can't help but moan as a jolt of pleasure shoots through me.

"Count," he says, his hand coming down on my ass again.

The sting of the spanking is intense, but it's mixed with a warmth that's spreading through my core. "You're insane."

"You're getting ten, but it doesn't start until you count."

"I'll go to campus security."

"You may do so once we're done here. Now fucking count."

He spanks me again, and I bite my lip to stifle a moan. The sound of his hand connecting with my flesh echoes in my ears, and I can feel the heat spreading across my skin. My body betrays me, and I can't help but squirm at the sensation.

"One," I finally manage to say, my voice barely above a whisper.

"Good girl," he says, his voice like dark velvet,

like black vellum, like everything soft and threatening at the same time.

He continues the punishment, each smack making me more aware of the heat building between my legs. "Two," I whimper. "Three."

"This is for being so fucking sexy," he says, his voice gruff against my ear. "For making me hard every time you walk into a room. For haunting my dreams."

Four. Five. Six.

I can feel the evidence of his arousal pressing against me as he leans over my back, his breath hot against my skin. His hand slides between my legs, his fingers teasing my sensitive flesh. "You're so wet, dear heart," he murmurs, a note of satisfaction in his voice. "You like this, don't you?"

Seven. Eight. Nine.

I can't deny it, not when my body is betraying me with every heartbeat. He continues to stroke me, each touch sending me closer to the edge. And just when I think I can't take it anymore, he spanks me the hardest, enough that I cry out, a sharp, high-pitched sound, before I can moan, "Ten."

I hear the sound of his zipper being lowered, the rustle of fabric as he positions himself behind me. "This is what you do to me," he says, his voice barely more than a whisper. "This is what happens when you defy me."

With a single, swift motion, he's inside me, filling me completely. Each thrust sends a jolt of pleasure mixed with pain through my body, the sensation of his cock rubbing against my spanked skin both intense and intoxicating.

I grip the edges of the study table, my knuckles white as I try to hold on. He's relentless, his rhythm steady and unyielding, driving me closer and closer to the brink. When I finally shatter, it's with a scream that echoes off the library walls, a wild, unrestrained sound that belongs as much to him as it does to me.

CHAPTER FOURTEEN

Learn Your Lesson

I'M STANDING ON a random corner on campus, one that's on the very edge. Campus is on one side of me. The other contains a strip mall with a Chinese restaurant and a frozen yogurt shop. They both do a brisk trade in student orders.

My ass throbs from the spanking. I should be outraged that Stratford thinks he can exert such control over me. The secret truth is that I've been aching with wetness ever since. He unlocked something inside me.

Something that wants to be hit over and over again.

Someone who wants to be protected at any cost, even violence.

It's not a healthy part of me, but then, I already knew I wasn't healthy. The deep research I've done into complex PTSD brought that into stark reality.

The evening air blows warm, but I still feel cold.

I had to jump through many hoops to get this far. Their invitations can't have anything as straightforward as a time and place. No, I had to scan a code that told me where to find a slip of paper under the third stepping stone of the art department's sculpture garden. The current task was to take a selfie at this exact intersection and send it to an unlisted number.

A sleek black limousine pulls up to the curb.

I hesitate, my heart pounding in my chest. The window rolls down, revealing the darkened interior. No one steps out to greet me. With a deep breath, I open the door and peer inside. The back of the limo is empty, save for a dark-tinted screen separating me from the driver.

A shiver runs down my spine, but I climb inside and close the door behind me. I sink into the plush leather seats despite the knot of anxiety in my stomach. Does every member of the Society get their own little scavenger hunt? Their own private limo?

It seems excessive, but then I suppose they love to be extra.

I have no idea where we're going. Or what's going to happen when we get there. The thought of being buried alive, or worse, digging up a potential corpse, sends a shudder through me. Though the Society would never be so gauche as to repeat themselves. Whatever I'm about to face will be new but no less perilous.

The limo turns a corner, and I catch a glimpse of the campus fading into the distance. My heart beats faster, the reality of my situation sinking in.

I'm at their mercy now.

There's no turning back.

The drive seems to last forever.

And it's over too soon, at the same time.

We pull up at some kind of mansion, like a massive antebellum plantation. It's surrounded by massive trees, their arms as thick as most trunks. Someone steps out from the mansion and opens the door.

I step out, my heels wobbly on the cobblestone driveway. "Hi."

The man has the posture and the distant expression of a butler. "Ms. Hill," he greets me with a nod, his voice as crisp as the autumn air. "Follow me."

We cross the threshold of the mansion, the grandeur of the interior matching the outside. This opulence might as well be a faraway planet. It's nothing I've ever experienced before. The butler leads me to a door at the back of the mansion, his steps echoing through the cavernous entrance hall.

He opens an ornate door and gestures for me to enter.

There's a stairwell and then darkness. A basement.

Of course it's in the basement.

As I descend, the door closes behind me with an ominous thud. The sound of a lock turning sends a jolt of adrenaline coursing through my veins.

Shit.

Voices hum somewhere ahead of me. At least I'm in the right place and not some random guy's basement. The sounds grow louder as I approach them in an underground labyrinth. I emerge into a vast, open space that's a far cry from any basement I've ever seen. These aren't walls built by man. They're left as nature made them. Cavern walls made smooth by water and eons.

Rich draperies adorn the stone walls in dark jewel tones. The room is filled with people, their chatter and laughter creating a disorienting soundscape. Some of them are dressed like you'd see at a high-end nightclub, in suits and short dresses. That's normal enough. They're not the terrifying part.

Because others are wearing hooded robes.

A shiver runs down my spine. The people in robes stand apart from the rest of the crowd, their faces hidden by shadows. Is that why they're wearing the robes, to hide their identities? Or is it something even more sinister, some kind of ritualistic costume?

The air runs thick with the scent of incense and candle wax. Flickering flames cast eerie shadows on the walls. It doesn't feel real, actually. It's like I've walked into a place where the lines between reality and fiction blur.

That's what the Society aims to do, after all.

Not to read Shakespeare, but to live it.

A few heads turn in my direction, their eyes assessing me with a mixture of curiosity and suspicion. A man detaches himself from the group of robed figures, his movements fluid and graceful despite the heavy fabric that cloaks his body.

He approaches me, his face still hidden in the shadows of his hood. As he draws closer, I can make out the contours of his features, the sharp line of his jaw, the fullness of his lips. There's an air of authority about him, a sense of power that's both intimidating and strangely compelling.

"Welcome, Anne Elizabeth Hill," he says, his

voice a low purr that makes me shudder. "We've been expecting you."

He says my name with a familiarity that feels like intimacy. "You might know my name," I say, my voice somehow steady, "but I don't know yours."

"I am Luca Andini, businessman, alumnus of Tanglewood University, and the president of the Society. And of course, a devotee of the Bard."

"If you're not a student anymore, then how can you still be a member of a college society?"

His eyes gleam with amused condescension. "The president," he says, correcting me. "Membership in the Shakespeare Society lasts a lifetime."

I don't like this guy, not his smooth words or his disdainful smile. "So you want to come back and party with co-eds? Creepy."

The corner of his lip lifts slightly, the barest hint of a sneer. "Parties? Games? Stunts? Those are only the entrance, the front porch. Once you get inside, you know that it's really about power."

"Only someone with no power gets off on lording over college kids."

His body tenses, and for a moment, my blood races. It feels like he might lash out physically, actually strike me. With what seems like a great effort, he relaxes. "My power rules over everyone. Over the humanities department. Over the university. Over Tanglewood City itself."

The implications of his words hang heavy in the air between us.

The Society isn't just a group of privileged students engaging in reckless hedonism. It's something much larger, much more sinister. The realization sends a cold shiver down my spine, but I force myself to hold his gaze, to not give him the satisfaction of seeing my fear.

I stand my ground, facing down the man who embodies the Society's hidden power, and I refuse to back down. "How would you control the city?"

Luca Andini watches me, his gaze sharp and assessing. "You'll see it for yourself soon enough, child."

"Don't call me child." The confidence in my voice masks a deepening fear. The Society's reach extends far beyond the ivy-covered walls of the university. They have their fingers in the very fabric of the city, wielding influence and authority in ways I'm only just beginning to understand.

"But you *are* a child. And you know my child." He waves a hand.

The crowd parts, and Matteo strides forward with the confidence of someone who's been bred for power and privilege. On campus he looks cocky and hot. But dressed in a suit that molds to his muscular frame, he exudes a menacing aura that sends a chill down my spine.

Matteo's icy gaze meets mine, and I see a flicker of something—surprise, curiosity, maybe even a hint of grudging concern. It's quickly masked by the same disdain he's always shown me. In front of his father, he's the picture of filial obedience, but there's an undercurrent of tension between them.

"I must prepare for tonight's entertainment," Luca says, leaving.

The moment he's out of earshot, Matteo's demeanor shifts. The hostility is still there, simmering beneath the surface, but it's tempered now, tinged with something that looks a lot like worry. "Why the fuck did you come tonight?" he hisses, his blue eyes boring into mine.

I don't trust him even a little bit, so no way am I going to tell him my real purpose. "I got an invitation," I say. "I thought it might be fun."

"The Society isn't about having a good time," he says, his tone harsh.

That's an understatement. "Yeah, I'm getting that."

"You have no idea what you're getting into."

He steps closer, his voice low and urgent. "It's not safe for you here. I tried to warn you away."

The memory flashes of him talking shit about my Tempest Prize entry in the Mayfair dorm. "Is that what you were trying to do?" I don't bother trying to hide my skepticism. "You should be clearer next time, because all it sounded like was you being an asshole."

Matteo runs a hand through his hair, frustration etched on his face. "I can't protect you," he says, his voice barely above a whisper.

A shiver runs through me.

Luca's voice rings out, commanding and filled with an unsettling fervor. "Esteemed members, excellent Shakespeareans, my erudite friends," he says, his gaze sweeping over the assembled throng.

Everyone gathers around a long, ornate table that dominates the room, the surface gleaming. The single chair sits at its head, adorned almost like a throne.

"We stand on the precipice of a new era, one where we will no longer remain in the shadows...no matter how much enjoyment we've found there." He pauses, and a ripple of self-congratulatory chuckles runs through the crowd. "Now we claim what's rightfully ours."

A cheer rolls up, echoing off the cavern walls.

I scan the faces around me, recognizing a few from the night I first stumbled upon the Society's revelries. I have no friends here. I'm glad Tyler didn't come, but I'm also painfully aware of how alone I am.

My gaze drifts over the robed figures standing off to the side, their identities obscured by their hoods. There's a sense of familiarity about one of them, a certain set of the shoulders that tugs at my memory.

As the figure shifts, a sliver of their face is revealed—full lips in red, a particular tilt of chin. My heart skips a beat. Professor Thorne. What's she doing here? She didn't even go to school here.

Matteo stands beside his father, his expression inscrutable. There's a tension in his posture, a rigidness that belies his calm exterior.

The applause fades, and Luca gestures towards the table with its lone chair. "Let us begin," he says, his voice ringing with authority.

The crowd parts, and a hush falls over the room as Luca makes his way to the head of the table. He settles into the chair with an air of regality, his eyes scanning the room with a predatory intensity.

Matteo hesitates for a moment, his gaze meeting mine across the room. There's a message in his eyes, a silent plea that I can't quite decipher. And then he steps forward, his movements fluid and deliberate as he approaches his father.

I hold my breath, watching as Matteo leans down to whisper in Luca's ear. The words are lost to me, but the look on Luca's face is one of satisfaction, as though he's just been given a gift he's long been anticipating.

As Matteo steps back, Luca's gaze finds mine once again. "Anne Elizabeth Hill," he calls out, his voice echoing through the silence. "Step forward."

Me? Why do they need me?

There have to be fifty, maybe even a hundred people in this place. I'm no one special. Which means that singling me out can't be a good thing. I take a tentative step backward, but people crowd behind me, forming a human chain.

Faces watch from the other side, some grinning with anticipation, others with a detached curiosity that's almost more terrifying than open hostility.

Luca's eyes lock on mine, gleaming with an unholy excitement.

I square my shoulders, lifting my chin in a vain attempt to project an image of defiance. I won't give Luca the satisfaction of seeing my fear, even if my insides are quivering like jelly. I'm acutely aware of the weight of the room's attention, the oppressive silence that hangs over the assembly like a shroud.

"What do you want with me?"

Luca's lips curl into a cold, cruel smile. "You thought we didn't know," he says, his voice carrying a note of darkness that sends a shiver of dread coursing down my spine. "You thought you could fool us. Expose us. And now, you will face the consequences of your actions."

My breath hitches in my throat as he leans back in his chair, the very picture of a monarch surveying his realm. How did he know? "What are you talking about?" The bluff sounds shaky. "I came hoping for free drinks."

"Strip," he says, the word like a knife.

"Are you insane?"

"Take off your clothes. Tonight you're going to be punished for your sins against the Society. You'll learn your lesson… And I'll enjoy teaching it."

A gasp escapes before I can stop it. "How dare you?"

A murmur runs through the crowd, a mixture of titillation and disapproval that makes my skin crawl. Their eyes strip me bare, and I have to fight the urge to wrap my arms around myself in futile armor.

Luca's smile never wavers, but there's a hardness in his eyes that wasn't there before. "You will do as you're told," he says, his voice like ice. "Or this will become harder on you."

The cavernous walls close in around me. Panic rises within me. I'm running out of space to breathe.

My eyes dart to the figure in the hooded robe, the one whose presence here fills me with a sense of foreboding. The curve of her shadowed red lips is unmistakable, a satisfied smile that chills me to the bone. Professor Thorne. Her betrayal cuts deeper than I could have imagined, twisting the knife of my fear until it threatens to split me wide open.

"You're sick," I hiss, my words laced with a mix of fear and defiance. "All of you."

Luca merely laughs. "Keep talking," he says, his gaze raking over me with open contempt. "You'll pay for every ounce of disrespect."

"I'll scream," I warn, my voice shaking with the effort it takes to keep it steady. "I'll fight you with everything I have."

"Good," he says, his voice unnaturally calm. "I enjoy a good struggle. It's healthy for a man to hold down a woman every so often, though with my looks and my power I do rarely have the opportunity."

My heart thrashes like a wild animal.

He's a hunter, the kind that toys with their prey.

The room is deathly silent now, the tension thick. Everyone's holding their breath, waiting for me to break. But I won't give them the satisfaction. I won't let them see my fear. They can do anything to my body, but they can't touch my soul.

I lift my chin. "Go to hell."

Luca's smile fades, replaced by a cold, calculating stare that sends a shiver of dread down my spine. "Very well," he says, his voice as icy as the grave. "Then you leave us no choice."

The words have barely left his lips when the room explodes into action. So many hands grip my arms, their fingers biting into my flesh as they drag me towards the center of the room. I struggle against their hold, kicking and screaming with all my might, but it's no use. They're too strong, too determined.

I'm powerless to stop them as they force me to my knees, their cruel laughter ringing in my ears as they leer at me, reveling in my humiliation. I feel a fresh surge of panic as they begin to pull at my clothes, their rough hands tearing at the fabric in their haste to carry out Luca's orders.

"Stop!" I cry out, my voice hoarse with fear and outrage. "Don't! Get off me."

They're beyond mercy, driven by a lust for power and a sick desire to dominate and humiliate. The sound of tearing fills the room, and then I'm naked.

I close my eyes, bracing myself for the ordeal to come.

It's a strange sensation, being mauled, being ripped apart. It's almost a surprise to find myself still in one piece as they shove me onto the table. Shivers overtake me, despite my resolve for them not to see my fear.

There's no escape, no salvation. I'm at the mercy of these monsters, and there's nothing I can do to stop it.

I cast a desperate glance around the room, my eyes pleading for help, for mercy, for anything that might deliver me from this nightmare. My gaze lands on Matteo, and for a fleeting moment, I see a flicker of something—pity? Regret?—in his eyes. But then he turns away, his jaw set in a hard line as he stares resolutely at the floor. He won't meet my eyes, won't acknowledge the terrified girl lying exposed on the table before him. He's as lost to me as the rest of them.

I'm alone in this, truly alone.

Luca approaches, his robe parting to reveal the unmistakable bulge of his arousal. The sight of it sends a fresh wave of terror coursing through my veins. It's not just the prospect of being violated that terrifies me; it's the realization that my fear is a source of pleasure for him. He's aroused by my suffering, turned on by my helplessness.

"Behave," he murmurs, his voice a silky purr that belies the darkness in his eyes, "and you might just make it through the night. You might even become one of us once you've suffered enough. Pain is an excellent teacher."

The way he says that makes me shudder. What did he teach his son? I can't feel sorry for Matteo, not when Luca trails up my leg, the touch of his fingers like ice against my skin.

I recoil from his touch even as I'm powerless to stop him.

My mind races with panic, with fear, I'm trapped.

He leans in close, his breath hot against my ear. "You're going to learn, Anne," he whispers, his voice filled with a dark promise that makes my blood run cold. "You're going to learn what it means to challenge the Society. And by the time I'm through with you, you'll beg to join us. You'll swear fealty to me if it's the last thing you do."

I squeeze my eyes shut, trying to block out the sound of his voice, the feel of his hands on my body. I could die. That's a truth I can't ignore. No one would even find my body. My parents wouldn't even miss me.

Luca slaps my breast, making me jump.

Tears prick my eyes. Sobs build in my throat. I'm losing the battle, surrendering to the hopelessness. But then, from somewhere deep inside, a spark of defiance flares to life. I may be at their mercy now, but I won't go down without a fight.

I grit my teeth and lash out with a kick. It's not very powerful, probably not graceful, but it lands on Luca's erection. Despite its thick erection, it feels sickeningly soft beneath my heel.

Luca gives a hoarse shout and goes down. I don't get the satisfaction of watching him fall as arms come to contain me, to drag me back. Someone has me in a chokehold while other hands hold my arms, my legs. Even more strike hard, painful, stinging blows on my body, fast retribution. I'm running out of air.

Some of the people in robes help Luca to his

feet. He looks deranged now, panting with pain, a grimace on his face. "You are going to regret that. Not right away. Slowly. After I fuck you, I'm going to pass you around. First with Matteo. Then with everyone else. And when your filthy cunt is too big and bloody, we'll switch to your ass. And when you're too disgusting to fuck, we'll use you to piss on."

I'm terrified and hurting, but all of it palls compared to my rage. I have nothing left to lose. "I must have forgotten which sonnet that was."

He's recovering enough that he doesn't look as pale. He steps forward, saying, "Spread her. Wider. I want to see the cunt I'm going to ruin."

CHAPTER FIFTEEN

The Prize

"DON'T TOUCH HER," says a voice, strong and commanding, cutting through the tension like a knife. The crowd parts, and there he is. Professor Stratford.

For a brief moment, intense relief steals my breath.

He's here to save me.

Except he barely spares me a glance, his gaze locked on Luca as he strides into the circle of onlookers with an air of undeniable authority.

Stratford's voice rings out, clear and resonant. "She belongs to me."

My breath catches in my throat.

He's not here to save me. Of course not. Because he's one of them. No white dress shirt or suit for him. He's in a freaking robe, belted by a rope, the hood thrown back. He's here to keep me all to himself, like a toy he doesn't want to share.

Luca's face contorts with anger, his eyes flashing dangerously. "If she's yours, then you can explain why she tried to expose us."

He stands there, unflinching, a small, knowing smile playing on his lips. "The invitation she received was not a regular one," he says. "It was a test, one I orchestrated so that I could be the one to punish her."

My mind reels. He's been manipulating me, stalking me, all along. He's admitting it, right here in front of everyone. And now, he's claiming ownership over me, as if I'm a prize to be won in their twisted game.

"It doesn't fucking matter," Luca says. "I'm president of the Society. Which means I can punish our enemies whenever I want."

A low rumble. "You dare to take what's mine?"

The air between them crackles with tension, the crowd holding its collective breath as they face off. Luca sneers, his eyes gleaming with malice. "If she belongs to you, then prove it."

Stratford turns to me, and for a moment, our eyes meet. There's a fierce possessiveness in his gaze that sends a shiver down my spine. "She's been mine all along," he declares, his voice dripping with conviction. "I arranged to mentor her for the Tempest Prize. I've been fucking her at every mentorship session."

Everyone snickers. A few guys whoop and holler. They sound young. Not one of the parents. One of the guys my age.

The world tilts under my feet. He's been pulling the strings this whole time, shaping my path, manipulating my choices. And yet, there's a part of me that can't help but feel a twisted sense of relief. He's here, claiming me as his own, and in this moment, it's the only thing keeping Luca's hands off me.

Is he any better than the monsters that surround us, or is he just another wolf in creepy Society clothing, fighting for the right to devour me?

Stratford's gaze never leaves mine as he steps forward, extending a hand towards me. "Come, Anne," he says, his voice leaving no room for argument. "It's time for your punishment."

The word hangs in the air, heavy with implications.

My punishment. At his hands.

Considering he already spanked me earlier, I'm not sure what else he might do. There's always the chance there is no punishment, that he's saving me, protecting me, but I'm afraid to believe it. The disappointment might hurt worse than his hand hitting my ass.

Hands release me, and I start to push myself up from the table.

"Don't fucking go anywhere," Luca says.

"You don't want to challenge me," Stratford says, his voice low.

Luca's smile is cruel. "It's not a challenge. She's yours, you say. Fine. Have the chubby little slut. But you forget, this isn't a personal punishment. It's for the entire Society to enjoy. Do it here."

Stratford's jaw clenches, the muscle pulsing in his cheek as he struggles to maintain his composure. "You want to watch me fuck her?"

Luca crosses his arms over his chest, his eyes glinting with a challenge that is both thrilling and terrifying. "If you want to prove your claim over her, to assert your dominance, it must be witnessed by the Society."

Stratford's gaze locks on to mine, and for a moment, I see a flicker of something that looks almost like regret. Then it's gone, replaced by the cool, commanding mask he wears so well. "Very well," he concedes, his voice betraying no hint of emotion. "Let the Society watch if it wants."

They close ranks around us, their faces a sea of

eager, predatory eyes. My skin crawls under their scrutiny, and I can feel the walls closing in on me.

Panic flares within me, bright and hot.

This can't be happening. Not like this, not in front of all these people. I take a step back, my eyes wide with alarm, but there's nowhere to run. The crowd has us encircled, their bodies a living barrier that holds me captive.

Stratford reaches for me, and instinctively, I recoil. We shared intimacy only hours earlier, but this is different. He is different—cloaked in the Society's robe, a stranger to me, a powerful figure who commands the room with an air of brutal authority.

With a swift, almost violent movement, Stratford pulls me close, his fingers digging into the flesh of my arm. The harshness of his action startles me, and I gasp, my eyes locking onto his in a silent plea for mercy. But there's no mercy to be found in his gaze—only a dark, consuming hunger that sends a shiver of dread coursing through my veins.

"Be a good girl, Anne," he murmurs, his lips a mere whisper from my ear. His voice is a low rumble that resonates deep within my core, stirring a mixture of fear and arousal that I can't quite suppress. "You can get through this."

I'm not sure I can.

He touches my breast in a firm, possessive hold. I wince, still tender from the slap Luca gave me. Stratford's eyes narrow. He moves to my other breast, caressing, somehow turning my nipple hard. How can I possibly find this arousing? I can't. I don't. I won't let him twist me this way.

I squirm in his grasp, a futile attempt to escape the relentless onslaught of sensation. But his grip is unyielding, his touch a brand that sears through my clothing, marking me as his. The crowd watches, their eyes avid, their breaths a symphony of hushed whispers and barely concealed moans.

He reaches down to test my readiness, rough fingertips circling my clit. I gasp. This is a violation. And yet, my traitorous body responds to his touch, heat pooling between my legs, readying itself for him. I hate myself for it, for the way my body betrays me, for the pleasure that builds within me.

"Look at you," Stratford says, turning to face the crowd. "Envious. Hungry. You were so desperate to watch me claim what's mine. Is that what power means to you? Your faces pressed to the fucking glass? I'll show you power."

They're rapt, their attention fixed solely on us, their expressions a mix of lust and jealousy. And in that moment, I understand the depth of Stratford's power, the control he wields over these people—over me.

He owns me, body and soul.

There's nothing I can do to escape his grasp.

He climbs on top of me, mounts me. It's animalistic.

Even though I'm completely naked, he doesn't remove the robe. It chafes against my skin, a coarse reminder of the brutality of this act. I'm pinned beneath him on the cold, hard surface of the table.

And somehow, my secret muscles clench.

He shouldn't have this effect on me—not here, not like this. He pushes aside his robe and slips inside me. It's faster than he usually goes with me. That thought rings like a bell through the illicit pleasure of it. He's already inside me, his cock filling me, stretching me, claiming me.

I close my eyes, trying to shut out the faces, the whispers, the shameful reality of what's happening. Then I feel Stratford's breath, warm against my ear, his voice a low, insistent murmur that shatters my defenses.

"Let them watch you come," he growls, the

rumble of his words somehow vibrating through my clit. "They wish they were me, fucking you, owning you. They're jealous, Anne. You're the one everyone wants. You're the prize."

The raw possessiveness makes me moan. Despite my fear, despite the eyes upon us, I am lost in the sensation of him moving inside me. He grinds the base of his cock against my clit until pleasure overwhelms my senses, obliterating everything but the feel of him.

My orgasm tears through me.

A sound of hoarse surrender tears from my lips.

His control shatters and he buries himself deep inside me with a final, shuddering thrust. His cry of release reverberates through the cavernous space, a triumph over the Society's power struggle.

For a moment, I am weightless.

The bliss of orgasm is a temporary relief.

Stratford withdraws from me, his weight lifting off my body as he stands. His cum leaks down my thigh. The reality of our situation comes rushing back. Nausea consumes me. I've just been used, displayed like a trophy for a room full of strangers. I lie there, exposed and shivering, my mind afire with self-loathing.

I can barely look at the faces surrounding us, their expressions a grotesque blend of lust and envy. Some of them have already started shedding clothes. Two girls are kissing. A guy holds a woman in front of him, his hands beneath her dress, her arms over her head. My body is still trembling from the aftershocks of my orgasm, a betrayal that leaves me ashamed. I've been on display, a spectacle for their amusement, and it's a violation as sharp and visceral as a blade.

Stratford stands beside me, his robe falling back into place with an air of casual indifference that makes my stomach churn. He looks out at the crowd, his gaze sweeping over them with undisguised contempt. "Scurry into your dark little corners and fuck each other," he announces, his voice carrying across the silent room. "It won't be as good as if you had her."

I'm not sure what to think.

He just forced me to have sex with him. Didn't he?

It seemed like he might be trying to help me, but it couldn't have been consensual, exactly, when my clothes are torn tatters on the ground.

Why would he taunt them if he's only trying to protect me?

Stratford turns to Luca, his eyes glinting.

"Don't ever challenge me again," he warns, his voice a low growl that resonates with authority. Luca's face hardens, but he doesn't argue. It's clear that Stratford has established his dominance over the Society and everyone present.

At least, for the moment.

Stratford may have manipulated and used me, but he also saved me from a far worse fate. My emotions are a tangled mess, a confusing blend of fear, gratitude, and a newfound vulnerability I can't seem to shake.

He somehow procures another robe and drapes it around me.

I shiver, not wanting to wear it, not wanting to be naked. There's no recovering my dress from the rags it's become.

"Come," he says, extending a hand towards me.

I can't bring myself to trust it. I hesitate, my eyes darting between his outstretched hand and the door that promises an escape from this madness.

"It's time to go," he says, his tone devoid of any warmth or tenderness.

I don't know where his loyalties lie, but it doesn't really matter.

He's my only escape.

CHAPTER SIXTEEN

Gilt Mirror

THE ROAR OF the engine fills the silence as Stratford navigates the winding highways of Tanglewood, his hands gripping the wheel with a quiet but unmistakable skill. Tension radiates off him, a stark contrast to the calm exterior he presents. The city lights blur past in a streak of neon, casting an ethereal glow over his features. And over my hands twisting in my lap.

I clutch the robe tighter around myself, acutely aware of the sticky residue between my thighs, a stark reminder of the power he holds over me.

The familiar skyline of Tanglewood's downtown comes into view.

It means we're nearing campus.

That should be a relief, and it is, but a greater part of me doesn't know how to move on from there. I'm no longer Anne, college student. I'm someone far more broken.

"What happened back there?"

"We'll talk about this when we stop," he says, his tone cool and detached. The dismissal stings, igniting a spark of anger that burns through the fog of my emotions.

"You don't get to tell me to wait," I retort, my voice growing stronger with each word. "What *happened* back there?"

His jaw tightens, a muscle twitching in his cheek as he navigates a particularly sharp turn at top speed. "Not now, Anne."

"Are you taking me back to the dorm?"

He chuckles, a humorless, mocking sound. "So everyone can see you in the robe and wonder what the Shakespeare Society did tonight?"

"Then where?"

He doesn't answer, his focus seemingly on the road, but I can see the tension in his shoulders, the rigid set of his jaw. He's making a decision, and it terrifies me that I have no control over what comes next.

The car continues to speed through the city, the world outside blurring into a sea of lights and shadows. I sit in silence, my mind racing as I try to anticipate his next move. The robe chafes against my skin, a constant reminder of my vulnerability, of the power he wields over me.

We end up at the Provost's house, a place I've been before.

I believed in Stratford then, believed he was helping Daisy, helping me. Then I learned the truth. I felt the lash of his cruelty. And I swore never to return. It just goes to show how little control I have over the situation.

Professor William Stratford is a man of both dominance and tenderness.

He shepherds me inside. I stumble along, not really knowing or caring. He holds out one of his dress shirts, all folded up. "The shower's in there."

Yes. A shower.

That sounds nice.

Except I'm not sure I can get through the mechanics of it all. I want to feel clean, wipe the soil of all those hungry gazes away, but the actual practicality of soap and water escapes me. I'm unraveling, thread by thread.

Stratford could say something cutting and cruel.

Instead he propels me into the bathroom with a surprising tenderness, his hand on the small of my back. He turns on the shower, adjusting the temperature, testing it with his hand. Such mundane things. Such practical things. Without a word, he reaches for the robe, his fingers deftly unknotting the rope at my waist. I flinch, but I don't move to stop him as the fabric pools at my feet, leaving me exposed.

Then he leads me into the shower.

Hot water cascades over my body, a cleansing torrent that I welcome. I want to breathe in the hot spray, to drown in it. Stratford lathers my hair with shampoo that smells like his coffee-colored locks. He rinses the suds from my hair, his touch soothing, almost reverent.

I can't help but gasp when his fingers slip between my legs.

He washes away the evidence of my defilement.

I close my eyes, lost in the sensation of his fingers tracing the contours of my body, mapping out the valleys and peaks of my form with a gentle thoroughness that leaves me both comforted and unnerved.

After that, he dries me and places me in the dress shirt, only half the buttons done. I'm cocooned in his shirt, settled onto an armchair, my hair still damp as he leaves to make a few low-voices phone calls.

He returns and picks me up in a strong motion.

I expect him to carry me into the bedroom,

and it's a surprise that I don't mind the idea. That's not where we go. Instead we end up in the office, its walls lined with bookshelves, each one crammed with leather-bound tomes and academic journals. A large oak desk dominates the space, its surface neatly organized with stacks of papers, a computer monitor, and an old-fashioned fountain pen set.

A Persian rug adds a touch of warmth to the polished wooden floor, and the room is illuminated by the soft glow of a green banker's lamp. In one corner, a high-backed armchair sits beside a floor-to-ceiling window, draped with heavy velvet curtains. It's a space that speaks of wisdom and tradition, a sanctuary where the pursuit of knowledge is both revered and relentless.

It's the place where I discovered his connection to the Society.

As he sets me down on the armchair, I catch my own reflection in a gilt mirror that hangs on one wall. My eyes are wide, my expression blank. Too blank, I think. This must be dissociation. I shouldn't be this calm.

After I'm settled, he kneels in front of me, one knee on the ground. If I were sitting instead of standing, this is the same pose we'd be in for a marriage proposal. Which is so far from whatever the fuck is happening here that it strikes me as funny.

A completely inappropriate giggle escapes.

Oh yeah, I'm definitely going insane.

Next I'll be singing about a baker's daughters and owls, like Ophelia.

"You asked me what happened," he says, his eyes dark and unfathomable. "It was assault. That's what happened. Don't let any of the other bullshit—the Society, our past relationship—hide that. You didn't want that."

I knew that but hearing the word hurts. "Why?"

"Because it was the only way to get you out of there safely." A rough laugh. "Safe. As if what I did to you doesn't matter. It's a terrible form of protection."

"I don't understand."

"They give everyone a special QR code. When Dean Morris tried to crack it in order to find them, they knew you'd given it to someone."

Oh God. "So I did this."

"No," he says, so sharp I flinch. He softens his voice. "They did this to you. I did this to you. And if you want to go to the police, I'll call them. Take you there. Tell them everything. Whatever you want."

Confusion. And then clarity. "You would do that?"

"Yes."

"Even though it would mean jail for you?"

His voice is hard. "It's what I'd deserve."

"It wouldn't bring down the Society, though, would it? They'd just blame it on you, distance themselves. My eyewitness account wouldn't matter. They never believe women, anyway. We'd have no proof of anything."

"A rape kit would show my DNA inside you."

His DNA. It's a strange way to think of his semen, even though of course it's true. It's a deeper intimacy even than sex, putting part of himself inside me, something that could be picked up even after a shower, even after those capable, strong hands washed me so thoroughly.

Except he didn't rape me. "You weren't there to help them, were you?"

A long beat passes. "No."

"You've been fighting them all along, haven't you?"

"Yes."

"So, in that basement…you were trying to protect me?" My voice is a whisper, barely audible in the quiet of the room. I think back to the night he pushed me away, the harsh words that cut through me like a knife. It all makes sense now—his sudden change of heart, his insistence that I stay away from the Society and its dangerous games.

He nods, his eyes meeting mine with an intensity that takes my breath away. "Yes," he admits, his voice raw with emotion. "I did it to protect you, but it doesn't change what happened. You were there against your will, and I made the choice to fuck you."

"I'm still glad you did."

"I'm sorry, dear heart," he says, his voice filled with a sincerity that I can't ignore. "I tried to keep you safe, but I failed. I never wanted you to get caught up in any of this."

He doesn't want absolution, doesn't want me to give weight to the fact that he didn't want to hurt me. My relief doesn't care. It's coursing through me. Even as he spat out terrible words to me in this very room, part of me struggled to believe it, didn't want to believe it. Refused to believe it. That's the only reason I could have had sex with him in that library.

"And Professor Thorne?" I ask, my mind racing with the implications of his confession. "Is she involved with them, too?"

Stratford's expression hardens. "She's on Andini's payroll. It's her job to find new recruits. And to make sure his son wins the Tempest Prize."

I think back to the competition in Thorne's class, the way she praised Matteo's analysis of *Hamlet*, the way she seemed to favor him over the other students. It was never about mentoring. It was about bribery.

I can't help but feel a sense of betrayal. Thorne had seemed so genuine, so passionate about her work. She's someone who found success in a male-dominated space. Why would she want to hurt a female student?

Stratford reaches out, his hand gently brushing against mine. "I know this is a lot to process," he says. "But I want you to know that none of it's your fault."

"Did you think it would come to this? When I was in your class?"

His voice is hoarse. "I told myself it wouldn't. I lied to myself about it, because the truth is I never should have touched you. I couldn't seem to stop, even knowing it wasn't safe for you. You're all I think about."

His words stir something deep within my core. Despite everything that has happened, despite the lies and the deception, I can't deny the connection that exists between us. There's a raw vulnerability in his eyes, a longing that mirrors my own.

"I found you by accident at the Pinnacle that first night," he says. "You captivated me, not just because of your beauty, but because of your passion for literature, your intelligence, your strength."

Warmth spreads through me, a mixture of desire and something more profound—a sense of belonging, of being truly seen by another person. "I don't understand why they even invited me."

"The Society may be power hungry and corrupt," he says. "But they do have a genuine love for Shakespeare. When they saw your potential, your promise as a scholar, it was only natural that they'd take an interest in you."

I look into his eyes, seeing the sincerity and the sorrow that lie within their depths. And in that moment, I realize that despite the pain and the heartache, despite the betrayal and the lies, I still care for him—deeply, irrevocably.

"It's not your fault," I whisper, my voice trembling with emotion. "You did what you thought was right. You tried to protect me."

He shakes his head, slow, refusing my forgiveness. "What can I do for you? What do you need? Anything, Anne."

I can't think about what I'm supposed to say. I've never been very good about fitting the mold, anyway. So I answer with the truth. "Hold me."

CHAPTER SEVENTEEN

Family Obligations

HIS TOUCH IS comforting, warm, strong, sending waves of safety coursing through me, returning me to my own body. I can also feel his erection.

"I'm sorry," he murmurs, his voice strained. "Please, ignore it."

He isn't touching me anywhere inappropriate. He sounds genuinely sorry, but he can't control it. And the truth is, neither can I. Despite the horrors of that cave, my body still hums with arousal because I'm in his arms. The pull between us is too powerful, too insistent. Too elemental.

I know it's messed up, but then everything about tonight has been messed up. Why should this be any different?

I lean in, pressing my lips to the column of his throat, tasting the salt of his skin. He's all masculinity and raw sex appeal, and I can't help but be drawn to him, despite the chaos that surrounds us.

"No, Anne," he says, his voice a low growl. "You don't want this."

I pull back, meeting his gaze with a fierce determination. "Yes, William," I say, using his first name on purpose. "I want you."

To prove my point, I take his hand and guide it to my breast, the one Luca didn't hurt. Stratford instinctively kneads and teases my nipple through the fabric of the shirt, sending shivers of pleasure down my spine.

With a look of tortured resignation, he pulls away.

"You're confused," he says. "You've been through a traumatic experience, and I can't take advantage of you."

"Don't infantilize me. I know my own mind."

Conflict rages in his dark eyes, the battle between his protective instincts and his own deep-seated desires. In that moment, I realize something profound: he's been hurt, too. The Society's twisted game forced him to do something unforgivable, something that went against his very nature.

He couldn't consent any more than I could. He had to do it to protect me. That's why he went faster. It wasn't enjoyment he felt on that table any more than my orgasm was genuine pleasure.

He was a victim in that moment, just as I was.

With newfound clarity, I climb into his lap, my knees straddling his hips. I pepper his face with soft kisses.

"Wait," he groans, resistance crumbling. "We can't."

"What happened before wasn't our choice. It wasn't even really sex. It was a show. Show me how beautiful it can be. I need to remember."

His response is visceral, a groan of surrender that resonates deep within my soul. His hands find their way back to my body, exploring and caressing.

His lips claim mine in a searing kiss. His hands, strong and sure, grip my waist, pulling me closer, as if he's afraid I might vanish if he lets go. The evidence of his desire, hard and insistent against my thigh, makes my mouth water.

There's no room for doubt or hesitation—there's only the overwhelming force of our mutual need. He lifts me effortlessly, this time turning me away from him, setting me on the side table so that I'm in front of the gilt mirror.

The position is intimate, exposing, and I can't

help but feel a flush of self-consciousness as my legs dangle over the edge, spread wide before him.

He stands behind me, his gaze locked with mine in the mirror even as he unbuttons the shirt and pulls it aside.

His fingers trace the column of my neck, a featherlight touch that sends shivers cascading across my skin. "This is yours," he murmurs. "Your strength, your grace, your intelligence."

His hands move lower, cupping my breasts through the fabric of my shirt. My nipples harden at his touch, aching for more. He brushes a hand to the side of the bruise left from Luca's hand, his expression darkening. "Your beauty, your power, your resilience."

His hands skim down my stomach to the insides of my thighs. I'm acutely aware of the heat pooling. "Yours," he says, husky with desire.

This isn't just about physical pleasure; it's a reclamation, a defiant stand against the claim that Luca and the Society tried to place on me.

With agonizing slowness, he parts the folds of my sex, revealing the flushed, aching core of me. I watch in the mirror, my breath hitching as I take in the erotic sight. "Look at how beautiful you are," he says, his gaze never leaving mine. "You are royalty, Anne. No one can take that from you."

His words wash over me, a powerful avowal of my agency.

"You're all I ever wanted," he murmurs against my temple.

His fingers begin to move, stroking and teasing with a skill that leaves me breathless, with a knowledge of me that feels reverent. Tension coils within me. Pleasure spirals higher. I arch into his touch, gasping as he kisses the side of my throat, nipping to make me jump and then licking to soothe it away.

I'm lost in a sea of sensation, every nerve ending alight. He's relentless in his pursuit, stroking the bundle of nerves. I cry out, my body bowing off the marble top of the side table as climax rips through me.

He doesn't stop, doesn't slow, not even as my body convulses around his fingers. I'm too sensitive, but he keeps going, bringing me to the edge and pushing me over again and again, each orgasm leaving me more mindless than the last. He's been hard against my back this whole time, groaning when I press against him in the throes of pleasure.

He nudges me back off the side table, supporting me with his strength. It's enough room for him to sheathe himself inside me. I'm a panting, quivering mess. Even so, the stretch borders on pain. I welcome it, welcome the feeling of wanting him, of choosing this.

He sets a punishing rhythm, his hips snapping against mine with an urgency that borders on desperation. I rock back thrust for thrust, our bodies moving together as one, each stroke of his cock hitting that perfect spot deep within me. The side table rocks ominously against the wall, threatening fracture. He doesn't seem to care. Neither do I. Let the entire city crumble around us.

The pressure builds once more. I cling to him, my fingers digging into the hard muscles of his back, as I shatter around him for what feels like the hundredth time. His release follows soon after, a guttural shout tearing from his throat as he spills himself inside me. He calls out my name, "Anne," a plea and a benediction all at once, his body shuddering against mine as he rides out the waves of his own climax.

For a moment, we stay that way, our bodies slick with sweat, our hearts beating in wild unison. He holds me close, his face buried in the crook of my neck, his breath hot against my skin.

In the aftermath, Stratford takes me back into

the shower again. I don't mind. I might never get enough of his hands soaping over me, feeling me, honoring me. Cleansing me in body and spirit.

We collapse onto the bed, falling into a deep sleep. It's nearly morning when we wake, dawn like a creeping tendril. I prop myself up on one elbow, looking down at him, his dark hair disheveled from my fingers.

"What now?" I ask, my voice barely above a whisper.

His eyes open, meeting mine with an intensity that sends a shiver down my spine. "I have to finish my mission, Anne," he says, his voice low and filled with an anguish that he tries to bury deep. "That's the most important thing. It's the only way to stop them. The only way you'll be fully safe."

Unease swirls in my stomach. "They'll come for me again?"

He reaches up, tucking a strand of hair behind my ear, his touch gentle yet firm. "I hope not. My claim on you at the Society meeting tonight should shield you, but you must not have any contact with them. None at all. Not even in classes. Ignore Matteo, ignore all of them. Pretend like you know nothing. That's the safest way for you."

A chill runs through me at his words. Their tendrils reach far and wide, their influence insidious and dangerous. But the thought of ignoring it all, of pretending like nothing happened, like I don't know the truth, seems impossible. "What about you?" I ask, my voice trembling slightly. "What's the safest way for you?"

His gaze darkens, a shadow passing over his features. "My path was set a long time ago, Anne. If I get harmed, or even killed, over the Society, it will only be just rewards for the sins I've committed in my life."

My heart aches at his words, at the resignation in his voice. "What terrible things have you done?" I ask, my voice barely above a whisper.

His jaw clenches. "I hurt you. Does anything else matter?"

"Yes."

"Fine, if you have to know, my father was the person who founded the society. This isn't only my past. It's his. He doesn't know what they're doing. Lost his mind a decade ago. Which was a relief, really. It would kill him."

I stare at him, my mind racing.

Pretending to be someone he's not in order to fulfill his family obligations—but it will ultimately result in his death. Like Hamlet. The thought sends a wave of panic coursing through me.

I don't know how to save him.

I don't think I can.

Reaching out, I trace the line of his jaw with my fingertips.

His eyes have closed, shutting me out. I'm left with a sense of dread, a gnawing fear that the man I've come to care for, the man I've chosen despite all the risks, is slipping away from me, drawn inexorably towards a fate he can't escape.

A knock comes at the door.

My heartbeat skips. Has the Society come for us?

Stratford doesn't look surprised. Instead, he rises and pulls on slacks before leaving to open the door. He comes back in with Daisy who has a tote bag and a look of concern.

"I brought you clothes," she tells me.

It's a reversal of the time last semester, when she was hurt by the Society. Now I'm the one lying in the Provost's house. She approaches me, her gaze softening as she takes in my state. I can't meet her eyes, can't bear the thought of seeing pity or judgment reflected back at me.

"How are you?" she asks, her voice gentle.

I offer her a small smile. "Oh, you know, a

little busy. Running errands, that kind of thing. Definitely no near-death experiences."

"Good," she says, allowing me to keep it light. "I would hate to find out you did something super dangerous and got hurt."

She helps me get dressed, which at first seems over the top, but as my movements are a little stiff, actually helps. Her movements are efficient, yet there's a tenderness to her touch that brings tears to my eyes. She doesn't push for details I'm not ready to share. Of all people, she understands that sometimes explaining something hurts as much as living it.

Once I'm dressed, she wraps an arm around my shoulders, guiding me towards the door. I cast a backward glance at William, who stands motionless by the window, his face a mask of unreadable emotions. Our eyes meet for a brief moment, and I see a flicker of something—regret, longing, despair—before he looks away, his jaw set in a hard line.

Daisy guides me back to the dorm, where absolutely no one takes notice of plain, boring, very studious Anne Hill, who probably went to some early TA study session. She would never go out late for a party. Never participate in some ritualistic forced group sex. My complete and total boringness is a shield.

The familiarity of our tiny room offers some comfort.

After all, nothing has really changed.

I'm just a broke scholarship student, living in the worst dorm on campus. And Stratford has an entire life where I don't belong.

CHAPTER EIGHTEEN
Heavily Guarded

THE CRISP MORNING air is a balm to my troubled thoughts as I meander through the verdant campus of Tanglewood University. The trees stand tall and proud, their leaves whispering secrets to the wind. I find solace in their silent company, their enduring presence.

I'm still trying to process the events of that night, of the Society's cruelty and my professor's confession.

As I navigate the cobblestone paths, my mind a whirlwind of emotions, I spot a familiar figure near the ancient oak that stands sentinel at the heart of campus. Professor Avery Miller, the esteemed scholar whose lectures on Greek myths captivated me, sits on a bench, her attention focused on the small creature scampering at her feet.

She's a striking figure, even from a distance.

Her blonde hair cascades down her back in loose waves, catching the morning light and setting it ablaze with fiery highlights. Her slender frame is draped in a tailored suit, the pale pink color feminine.

She wears minimal makeup. It makes her seem younger than other female professors. It also makes me wonder if she gets underestimated because of it.

A fat squirrel waits for her to toss what appears to be the very last piece of her bagel. She laughs as he grabs it, only moving away a few feet before nibbling. Campus squirrels are bold. And legendary. There's one who hung out around the west quad that people swear could work a vending machine.

I shouldn't bother a professor on her break. It's bad form. Then again, it's not like I can really attend office hours either. The classics elective I took last semester is likely the only one I'll ever have with her.

She teaches some others, and I'd love to take them, but the scholarship doesn't allow for trying things out. It's strictly necessary for graduation only.

And yet, there's something about her that invites approachability, a warmth radiating from her that's both comforting and commanding.

While I'm standing there like a stalker, she notices me and raises her hand in a wave.

"Anne, please tell me you have carbs or nuts in that tote bag. The Sciuridae population on this campus are at risk of starvation."

I grin. "I may or may not have a contraband muffin, but it's from Hathaway, and they have turned their nose up at such offerings before."

Hazel eyes twinkle. "The Mayfair muffins must have a superior nutrient factor."

"Yeah, or they use actual butter and milk."

"Or that," she agrees.

"What did you call them? Scurry-something?"

"The Sciuridae family includes squirrels, chipmunks, and prairie dogs. It comes from the Greek word *skiouros*, which means shade tail."

She specializes in Greek mythology. "Was that in an extant text?"

"Nah, I looked it up on Wikipedia one afternoon while I was out here. Come sit down. There's plenty of room."

I hesitate for a moment, but the kindness in Avery's eyes beckons me forward. I join her, my mind torn on what to ask—if anything.

"How's the semester going?"

"To be honest, not great."

"I'm sorry to hear that. Is there anything I can do to help?"

"Actually, I wonder if I could ask a question about…you?"

Her eyebrows rise. "Let's hear it."

I know I should be worried about the Society's plans for global, or at least university domination. And I am. Though the part that keeps replaying is the hooded Thorne's smile. She certainly would never have invited a student to sit on a bench with her. Or even feed the squirrels. She would be too busy achieving. I thought I wanted that, too.

Not at the expense of integrity.

"I've always wanted to be in academia, like you. There was never even a plan B. But lately I've been wondering… How it is to be a woman?"

"Ah, that."

I can't help but smile at her wry tone. "That bad, huh?"

"I'm not going to sugarcoat it. Women are underrepresented in the tenure track, but disproportionately represented in unranked instructor positions."

"In other words, they want women to teach while the men get to do the research, write their books, and speak at conferences."

"And even when they do make professor, there's a pay gap."

"I can't believe we still have to deal with that."

"Inherent bias is hard to uproot. Worse are the people who say the gap only exists because women are inherently less qualified."

"Is there any good news?"

"It's more of lateral news. These gaps exist in all industries. Academia is not an exception. It's only more offensive because you'd assume they would know better since they care about knowledge, but ironically knowledge is one of the most heavily guarded areas in the patriarchy."

"Because the more knowledge women have…"

"The more powerful. Exactly."

"So maybe a better question is how do you live in such a tilted system without going insane?"

"Sometimes just existing, taking up space, doing the work you love, is an act of rebellion."

"I like that."

"Though other times you might let yourself go a little insane. As a treat."

I laugh, but then my smile fades. "I guess I'm more concerned about turning bitter. Or catty. Or becoming one of them."

My words feel nebulous out of context, but

Professor Miller seems to understand. "Women are some of the worst offenders of the patriarchy. They think they have to act like a man to succeed or push down other women."

I've been dreading Professor Thorne's class this afternoon. That's exactly what she's like. "Have you worked with people like that?"

"Oh, I still do. I take some private pleasure in calling out their bullshit in the context of ancient Greek mythology, but the truth is, they're not going to change. See that squirrel? He fights away the others, even though he's already full, even though campus has more than enough bagels to go around. He feels like it's necessary to his survival."

"So even though he gets plenty of food, he feels like he's fighting for his life?"

"Exactly."

The quiet praise in her tone makes me feel ten feet tall. It's a reminder that you don't need to act like a hard-ass to teach, to inspire, or to be taken seriously.

"Even though these squirrels are basically rodent billionaires, the epitome of privilege in their world, they're still operating on old software."

"I don't suppose there's a mandatory system

update we could push out?"

She smiles. "Maybe your engineer friend can work on that. How is she, by the way?"

Professor Miller was there the night we found Daisy half dead. She's been conversing in hushed, urgent tones when Professor Stratford and his brother, Cormac, who's also a professor on campus. "I wish I knew."

Her expression fills with sympathy. "A friend of mine does his research on higher education social groups. Mostly fraternities and sororities, but also secret societies."

"What does he think of—" I stop myself before saying the name out loud. It feels like I'm being watched. There are eyes everywhere. "What does he think of them?"

"I asked for his help on this. He said these are more than social groups. They're essentially networks designed to build power. You know how cheerleaders build a pyramid one person at a time? The person at the top gets higher than they could have alone."

That explains Luca Andini's reasoning but not Professor Thorne's. "What about the person who's at the bottom of the pyramid? She's no higher than if she stood alone."

"Perhaps she's blinded by the pageantry of it.

Or she doesn't want to be alone. You might be surprised at how strong of a motivator that is. Or many times she thinks she can climb her way to the top one day. Even if she's wrong, it's enough to keep her in the pyramid."

That sounds like Professor Thorne.

She frowns. "They aren't still bothering Daisy, are they?"

No, they've moved on to me. But I don't want to burden her. "No, she's done with them. Thank goodness. I should get going. My class starts soon."

She smiles, though it's a little speculative, as if she can sense my withholding. "The academia needs women like you. Bright. Curious. Brave enough to challenge the norms. You can always come to me, Anne. Whether you need advice or someone to listen."

"That means a lot to me."

As I stand to leave, a chill runs down my spine. The feeling of being watched returns with a vengeance, a silent warning that our conversation has not gone unnoticed. I turn to look behind me, half expecting to see a member of the Society lurking in the shadows.

But there's nothing—just flower petals blowing in the breeze.

I slip into the lecture hall just as the bell tolls, signaling the start of Professor Thorne's class. The room buzzes with the low hum of whispered conversations, the sound tapering off as Thorne strides in. I make my way to the seat next to Tyler. He looks much better after his encounter with the Society. His body seems healed, but his spirit still seems low.

I settle into my chair, my heart pounding a staccato rhythm against my rib cage. The sight of Professor Thorne, with her sharp features and commanding presence, sends a jolt of adrenaline coursing through me. It's her—the woman from the Society's event. The certainty fans the embers of fear and anger nestled within my chest.

Thorne launches into her lecture, her voice a rich contralto that fills the room. She discusses Ophelia's death, her words painting a vivid picture of the tragic scene. As she delves into the nuances of Gertrude's role in the play, something within me snaps.

Unlike Stratford and most other upper-level instructors, Thorne doesn't want us to have our own opinions. She presents the ideas and tells us which one is the best.

In the case of Ophelia's death, she's pushing the more bizarre idea that Gertrude imagined the entire episode, that it's part of the mythos. Except Ophelia had seemed real enough in her other scenes.

I can't sit here in silence, not when she's twisting the truth for her own ends. Not when she's the one who watched that night's horror. I raise my hand, my fingers trembling with a mixture of nerves and indignation. Thorne's eyes flicker to me, a hint of annoyance passing over her features.

She turns her face away, ready to ignore me.

So I stand, my legs unsteady beneath me. "Professor Thorne," I say, my voice steadier than I feel. "Gertrude specifically mentions her reflection in the water. That detail makes it unlikely as a random story. It also proves she could have saved Ophelia if she wanted to. So why did she let her die?"

A murmur ripples through the class, and out of the corner of my eye, I see Tyler's brows knit together in concern.

Thorne's eyes narrow. "This is not an open forum, Ms. Hill. I'm teaching the correct interpretation, not whatever you thought of while you took a shower this morning."

"Maybe she was afraid that Ophelia had seen and heard too much. She was a threat to the entire throne…and therefore a threat to Gertrude herself, who benefited the most from the royal privileges."

Her lips press into a thin line. "You will see me in my office after class."

The rest of the class passes in a blur.

When the lecture finally concludes, I gather my belongings and make my way to her office. I'm trembling, though it's not really nervousness. It's not even rage. It's an overload of emotion. Or in scientific terms, my amygdala's releasing adrenaline, because it knows I'm preparing for a fight.

I walk down the hallway towards Professor Thorne's office, my heart pounding in my chest. I don't know what to expect, but I know that I need answers. The image of the woman at the Shakespeare Society initiation is still fresh in my mind, and I need to know why she was there.

I knock on the office door.

Thorne's voice summons me inside.

The walls of her small, windowless office are practically wallpapered with her published work, her awards. They're clearly attempts to bolster her authority. It makes me sad, the way she's trying to overcompensate.

She stands in front of her desk, arms folded across her chest. "You interrupted my lecture today. It was unprofessional and disrespectful. Speaking out of turn will not be tolerated."

"Neither will the truth, apparently."

"Your interpretation of *Hamlet* is flawed, and your outburst was inappropriate. You owe me an apology."

"You understand Gertrude's point of view, don't you?"

"I have no idea what you're talking about."

"Don't you? I think you know all about letting a young woman drown because she threatens the centers of power that benefit you."

She narrows her eyes, red lips pressed together.

The same red lips that had been under the shadowed hood.

"You were there," I say. "You watched while they tore off my clothes. While they dragged me onto that table. You were *smiling*."

Her eyes flash. "I don't know what deranged dreams you've been having, but if you persist in saying such inappropriate things to me, I'll have no choice but to contact campus security."

"Call them. I'll explain what happened. You don't have an alibi, do you?"

Thorne leans back against her desk, her arms folded. "Assuming, for a moment, that I was there, what would you have me do? Turn against my own colleagues? Risk my career and my reputation for an upstart little slut?"

"No, I suppose someone like you could never do that."

"I told you the first day of class that none of it mattered to me. Whether the children in my class like me. Whether other professors like me."

"Yes," I say, my tone mocking. "You're here for the work. For the study. For Shakespeare. But you don't actually care about that. All you care about is power, even if it means fucking the head of a secret society to get it."

It was a guess, and judging from the high color in her cheeks, it was correct. "Get the fuck out of my office. And hope like hell I don't fail you."

"I don't think you'll do that. I don't think you'll want to explain how someone with all As in all my classes ever suddenly failed. It would be awkward for you."

Her silence is my answer. I turn to leave, my heart heavy with the weight of betrayal. As I reach the door, I pause, glancing back at Thorne. Her eyes are fixed on the floor, her body as rigid as armor.

"I wanted to be like you—strong, successful,

respected."

"You will *never* accomplish what I have."

"I know." And it's the truth. She means the accolades papering the wall, but I mean the way she's traded in integrity to get them. If I am lucky enough to get those things, it will be on merit. And if the world is determined to shut me out, then I will still love Shakespeare. I'll still study and think and write. Because it was never about being lauded. It was always about the work.

CHAPTER NINETEEN

Pissing Contest

THE TEXAS LANDSCAPE blurs into a haze of greens and browns from the bus. Daisy reclines beside me, her head resting against the window, her blue eyes reflecting the passing scenery. We point out the cows each time we pass them. We're heading home for spring break. To my home, specifically.

Daisy suggested we make this trip together.

To be honest, I'm not sure whether she's doing it to avoid her family or to support me with mine. She claims it's going to be like a field trip for her anthropology class with Professor Avery, to see how my crazy family lives.

The bus pulls into Port Lavaca. The familiar dread overtakes me. The town is small, the kind of place where everyone knows your business before you do. My parents live on the outskirts, in a run-down house that's seen better days. Rusty, our old dog, greets us with squinty eyes and a wagging butt.

My father raises an eyebrow at Daisy. "You say you're studying engineering? Ain't that dangerous, what with all the wires?"

"Yes," Daisy says, her expression completely solemn. "I wear a helmet whenever I have to go up in the articulated boom lift."

I manage not to crack a smile as she describes working for a telephone company, instead of the edge of nanotechnology that she loves.

"You're so skinny," my mother says. She has no boundaries, so she accompanies these words with pats on Daisy's arms and hips. "Are you sick, dear? I have the hardest time keeping food down, you know."

Daisy, bless her, chats with my parents, asking them about their lives, their opinions, as if they're the most interesting people she's ever met.

She charms them, which is not really a surprise.

The surprise is that they actually settle into something resembling half-decent behavior. My mother reclines on the sofa with her pained martyrdom. My father sits in his recliner, a blank smile plastered on his face.

There's only one tense moment, when my

mother asks me for money. Her new medicine helps, but it's a brand name. Five hundred dollars a bottle. Even knowing it's a lie doesn't help my shame that I can't give it to her.

"I don't have any money," I say honestly.

My father slams his hand on the table, making everyone jump. "You could be here earning money for her treatment. You go off reading books, letting her die, because you never did give a shit about family."

I flinch at the harsh words. I've heard them before, but somehow they hurt every time. Though no tears fall. A long time ago my body realized it would be a waste of resources.

Daisy defends me. "She's working so hard at school, doing what almost no one else could do. Getting As in classes that everyone else struggles with."

My parents stare at her like she's speaking another language.

They don't understand, don't *want* to understand, but I appreciate the attempt. Sometimes I dream of saying a few things to her family. Most likely the same thing would happen. They don't have any empathy.

She and I explore the town together during the day. I take her to the high school, the library, the diner where I waitressed—my usual haunts. I also show her the place where seniors set off firecrackers behind the bleachers for their prank, the grove where people park their cars to make out, the community center, where people gather over bingo cards to complain about the youths.

She has this ability to make friends everywhere she goes. I always knew about it, but it's different seeing it on campus compared to the town. It's not like people were mean to me here. If anything, I got my share of sympathy for my parents. Everyone knows about the Hill family. But I rejected anything that seemed like pity. And I suspect that I might have taken genuine overtures of friendship or kindness that way, too.

I watch her ask questions about the thirty varieties of tomato that Mrs. Ferguson grows, a smile at my lips. Her enthusiasm is infectious, and for a moment, I almost care about the various water content or flesh thickness of the fruit-slash-vegetable. It occurs to me that everyone has their own version of Shakespeare, something they're obsessed with, something that has value…not only for them, but for the world.

At night, we share my bedroom, taking turns on the bed and the old, moth-eaten sleeping pad, whispering in the dark things that would be too hard to say in the light. Things like how I miss Stratford, even though I shouldn't. Things like how she hurts thinking about her family, but she knows she'll go back.

Rusty passes back and forth between us, providing comfort to whichever one of us needs it, pressing his face into our necks, his fur absorbing our tears until we can laugh it off once again. He's a godsend.

He's also turning so gray. It hurts to look at him, to know I'm missing the final years or even months of his life. Life is about choices. I could stay with him, but I'd lose myself. I suppose the same is true of Stratford.

Which just proves what my childhood taught me.

Love is not a good thing. It's deep water. And the worst part is, we put the chains on ourselves and sink to the bottom.

Daisy and I also clean the house.

That's my job, and I can't skip it even with a guest.

The house is spotless now, every surface scrubbed, every corner dusted. It's a futile attempt to cleanse the space of the toxicity that lingers in the air. Daisy had thrown herself into the task alongside me with a determination that I both admired and found embarrassing.

"I told you not to come," I say, my voice tinged with regret.

She waves me off. "Gotta get rid of the calories somehow."

I roll my eyes, because she probably weighs half as much as me. "Don't get rid of any calories. You are literally the perfect shape."

She snorts. "Don't tell me you're mad about your curves, the ones that make your professor get all hot and bothered—"

"Stop right there," I interrupt, my cheeks flaming. I glance towards the closed door, paranoid that my parents might overhear.

Daisy grins, her dimples on full display. "Sorry not sorry."

As I sit there, surrounded by the familiar walls of my childhood bedroom, I'm reminded of just how far I've come—and how much further I still have to go. Daisy's presence is a comforting one, but it's also a stark reminder of the secrets I'm keeping. We'll return to Tanglewood soon, and I'll be thrust back into the tumultuous world of academic competition, illicit affairs, and secret societies.

On the last night, we make our way to a local bonfire.

Daisy's in her element, laughing and chatting with a group of locals as if she's known them all her life. I envy her ability to adapt, to find joy in the companionship of others.

I've never known how to do that.

I wander away from the firelight, the darkness of the woods enveloping me like an old friend. My phone screen contrasts with the natural gloom around me. I open the online program where the latest draft for my paper waits.

As I start to reread it for the millionth time, I notice another icon in the document. He's here, reading it, too. Adrenaline jolts through me. The thought of him being here with me, even though we're miles apart, thrills me.

It also terrifies me, how connected I feel.

The paper is basically done. I might change one single word every time I read through it, sometimes one as small as a preposition. The limit of three thousand words means that every single one counts.

I've cited a study that proves that prolonged objectification contributes to psychological trauma, as well as depersonalization. Ophelia becomes a spectator in her own life.

At her funeral, Hamlet and Laertes fight over who loved her more, but it's performative. Neither actually knows her. She is an object to them, even in death.

I press enter and type, *Essentially, it's a pissing contest.*

He only has access to read and comment. That's what he does now, adding a note on the new sentence. *Insightful. Accurate. Lacking the pedagogical language that will make this accepted in academia.*

I grin. I'm going to erase the line in a minute, but I'm enjoying this. Even though I probably shouldn't. There's nothing romantic about editing a document together, is there? I delete *pissing contest* and replace it with *an unproductive competition driven by pride, where participants assert authority over one another using archaic or harmful metrics.*

Better, he adds in a new comment. *Though now you're over word count.*

I delete the sentence altogether, but reply to this comment. *Sometimes pedagogical language is not better. It's just longer.*

Blasphemous, he replies. *And accurate.*

Branches rustle. Feet whisper over the loamy earth.

Red, one of the local guys, his girlfriend, a sweet, doe-eyed girl whose name I can't quite remember. They settle down near me, their voices barely more than a whisper. I hold my breath, hoping they won't notice me. My heart sinks as they begin to kiss, murmuring sex words, love words. My cheeks burn.

I swallow hard, my mind racing as I try to think of a way to escape without being noticed. But then the girlfriend speaks. "I'm pregnant."

There's a long pause, and then Red's voice comes too low to understand. It's almost as low as the vibration of the earth. It's urgent, too. And…somehow I can tell, full of promises. That's what's happening right now. A family is being made. That should be sweet. It *is* sweet, but a shiver runs down my spine.

This is what happens to girls who stay in Port Lavaca.

Getting pregnant. Getting married. Often in that order.

I never wanted that.

Which is why I need my degree. I need the Tempest Prize. It's not a game to me. It's my escape pod from this adorable and stifling small town. There's only so long I can watch my life as a spectator. This is how I break free.

CHAPTER TWENTY

Poetry for a Living

THE LAST MENTORSHIP session feels the most remote, the most stilted. There's too much beneath the surface to be anything but polite and professional. The weight of our shared secret hangs heavy in the air.

We meticulously comb through my paper, refining every argument, every sentence until it shines. The words we craft together are sharp, poignant—a testament to our combined intellect, a dance of wits that leaves me both exhilarated and emotionally drained.

I can feel the electricity crackling between us, a dangerous current that threatens to pull me under. But I refuse to succumb. I've come too far, worked too hard to let my guard down now. So I pull back, cloaking myself in a layer of icy detachment. I focus on the work, on the words on the page, on the way my arguments unfold with precision and clarity.

Stratford seems to sense the change in me, but he doesn't press. Instead, he matches my remote demeanor, his own walls rising as he concentrates on our task. We are two scholars, working side by side, nothing more, nothing less. The silence between us is punctuated only by the tap of my foot as he does the final read-through.

"Perfect," he says.

"Really?"

"It's brilliant. Truly. You deserve to win."

The words hang in the air, a validation of all the late nights, the endless research, the moments of doubt and despair. I want to thank him, to tell him how much his approval means to me, but I can't find the words.

They wouldn't be appropriate, anyway.

"But I won't. Right?"

He sighs. "Thorne doesn't control the board of this award…but she has influence. Her father does, too. And I suspect she did more than just advise Matteo. She would have fed him whatever she thought would win."

"Right." My voice comes out hollow.

"It doesn't mean anything."

It means everything. The fact that good work won't count. The fact that it's about who you know, which he told me before. I didn't want to believe him then. "I'll keep that in mind while I clap for Matteo."

I gather my things with firm, almost too-hard movements. The distance grows between us, a necessary barrier that will protect me. I rise from my chair, slinging my bag over my shoulder, ready to face whatever comes next—alone.

As I reach the door, I pause, casting one last glance back.

Stratford sits there, his gaze fixed on the space where I stood just moments before. There's a vulnerability in his eyes that I've never seen before, a flicker of something deeper.

I should leave. It would be the smart thing to do, the safe thing. I've already risked too much by staying this long, by allowing myself to get caught up in the storm of desire that surrounds Professor William Stratford. With the mentorship over, I'm free of it. But as I stand at the threshold of the bookshelf, I can't bring myself to walk away.

His normally impenetrable demeanor shows signs of wear.

He looks a little…sad.

That shouldn't matter to me, but it does.

I let go of the doorknob and take a step back into the room. "What's wrong?" I ask, my voice softer than I intend it to be.

He glances up at me, his expression quickly hardening into a mask of indifference. "Nothing," he says, his tone dismissive. "You should leave."

I know him too well now. "Something's bothering you. And it's not how amazing my concluding paragraph was."

He doesn't smile. "You need to leave."

A shiver runs through me. "I'm not scared."

"This is your last warning."

"Not going anywhere."

"Do you really want to be fucked by me that badly?"

His words feel like a slap in the face, even though I recognize them for what they are. He's trying to push me away. They're a form of protection, the same as my isolation. "You know, I'd really think someone who studies poetry for a living would understand emotions better."

Something flickers across his handsome face, grudging respect for my tenacity, acknowledgment that I scored a point. "If we understood it, we wouldn't need poetry so much."

"So what are you feeling?"

"I'm feeling like I'd fuck your smart mouth."

"Then I guess we're at an impasse," I say, my voice steady despite the adrenaline coursing through my veins. "Because I want more than that from you. Then again, maybe we can both get what we want."

He watches me with wary eyes as I drop to my knees in front of him, my hands deftly working the buckle of his belt. His breath hitches as I unzip his slacks and free his already hard cock, the evidence of his desire for me both a victory and a reminder of the complex game we're playing.

I need to taste him, to feel him in my mouth, to serve him in this most intimate of ways. It's not about love or even lust.

It's about power and control. I want to give him both.

And then take them away.

His cock is already hard, straining against the fabric of his slacks. I undo his belt and zip with practiced ease, my fingers trembling with anticipation. When I finally free him from his confines, I can't help but let out a low moan at the sight of him. He's so beautiful, the thick length, the dusky head, the pearl of wetness at the tip.

I lean forward, my lips brushing against the tip of his cock.

He shudders.

A lick reveals that salty, addictive flavor. I take

him deeper into my mouth, my tongue swirling around his shaft as I suck him.

He groans, his hands tangling in my hair as he guides himself deeper. His cock throbbing against my tongue, but it's far too soon for that.

I look up at him, my lips still wrapped around him. He's watching me with something that looks like awe. It's intoxicating, knowing that I have this effect on him. I suck hard, and his hips buck as he fucks my mouth. My body responds to the primal energy of him, getting slick and soft between my legs.

But I can't let myself get lost in it.

I need to stay focused, to keep my mind on the task at hand.

This isn't about me. Or even him. It's about control.

His hands grip my hair tighter as he thrusts deeper into my mouth.

The taste of him is intoxicating, a heady mix of salt and skin that makes my head spin and my core ache with a need that's become all too familiar. I savor the sensation of his thickness sliding against my tongue, the way his body responds to my touch—a dance of power and vulnerability that sends shivers down my spine.

I'm lost in the rhythm of it, the wet sounds of

my mouth around him, the soft, desperate noises he can't help but make.

His thighs tense beneath my hands, the muscles quivering with the effort to hold back, to maintain some semblance of control. His moans fill the silence of the library's upper floor, a symphony of desire that echoes in the hollow space around us.

I know he's close, teetering on the edge of release, and the knowledge thrills me, fuels my own aching need.

Before he can come, I pull away, his cock slipping from my lips with a wet pop. I sit back on my heels, reveling in the frustration that washes over him.

"Don't stop," he says in a low rasp.

I meet his order with a steady gaze, my resolve hardening even as my body protests. "Then tell me what's wrong," I say, my voice firm despite the trembling in my limbs.

He averts his eyes, his jaw clenching as he shakes his head. "It's nothing," he insists, his tone laced with a desperation that betrays his words.

I lean forward, my hand wrapping around the base of his cock, my thumb teasing the sensitive spot just beneath the head. His breath catches, his hips jerking involuntarily as I stroke him, my grip just firm enough to reignite the fire I've so cruelly doused.

His control is slipping, his composure unraveling with every stroke, every swirl of my tongue, every gentle squeeze of his balls. I take him deep again, relishing the way he swears under his breath, the way his fingers tangle in my hair, pulling just hard enough to make my scalp tingle.

And then, just as his body begins to tremble again, I pull back once more, leaving him shaking, gasping for air, on the brink of ecstasy.

"Fuck," he says.

"Tell me," I whisper, my lips grazing the damp tip of his cock. "What's wrong, William?"

His response is a guttural growl, a wordless plea for release. A visceral response to my temerity at using his first name. I hold my ground, my gaze unyielding, my determination a fortress around my heart. Though the fortress walls are crumbling.

I'd really think someone who studies poetry for a living would understand emotions better.

The same is true for me, of course. I've never understood emotion. That's how I've ended up at this man's feet, thinking I'm not halfway in love with him.

Again and again, I bring him to the edge, only

to withdraw, leaving him panting, begging, reduced to a creature of pure need. I revel in the power I wield over him, the control I exert with every flick of my tongue, every caress of my hand.

If we understood it, we wouldn't need poetry so much.

He's become poetry, his tremble the rhythm, his curse words the symbolism, the wetness between my thighs the irony.

I see the moment his resolve crumbles. He's exposed, stripped bare by the relentless onslaught of pleasure and denial. His eyes are dark with desperation. And though he's defeated, he also seems relieved. As if he wanted this. Needed it.

I release him, sitting back on my heels as I wait for him to speak. His chest heaves with each ragged breath, his body still shaking with the aftershocks of his denied release.

"I'm worried about Brandon," he says, his voice hoarse. "Dean Morris asked me to come back, to clear out the Shakespeare Society. I never wanted to return. The only reason I did is because Brandon is here."

"He's part of the Society?"

"Not really. He joined when they invited him, but he doesn't give a shit about Shakespeare. They don't want him because he likes literature. They targeted him because of my history."

"Like retaliation?"

"More like they thought if they could get Brandon to side with them, they'd have more power in the Society. I have to destroy them, not only for the school, but for my son. I haven't been there enough for him. This is my chance to make amends."

His words make me shiver. The vulnerability in his words strips away the layers of professor and student, of lover and mentor.

We both care about Brandon, though in different ways. I might not be close to him, but I don't want him to be consumed by the Society.

It's a strange sensation, to be kneeling before him, his cock still glistening from my attention, as we discuss the well-being of his son—a young man I once thought I could have been with.

A strange sensation, but then our reality has always been complex. Twisted.

It's always been forbidden, but it's ours.

Words can't fix this, so I don't offer empty promises.

Instead I give him comfort the best way I know how.

I take him into my mouth.

He groans a prayer, a promise. His hips buck

beneath me as he loses himself in the sensation. He's on the edge again, his entire body quivering with that almost-climax. I don't pull away this time. I suck him harder, allowing him deeper into my throat, swallowing around him until he shouts.

His thighs vibrate with power as he spills himself onto my tongue. It's a moment of pure ecstasy, a shared victory against the worry that's been haunting us. I don't fool myself into thinking that a blowjob has managed to solve anything. Or that these problems are even solvable. There's solace to be found, though. Even in the darkest times, we can find respite, a moment of raw, blinding, carnal light.

CHAPTER TWENTY-ONE
Position of Authority

'M FILLED WITH a sense of well-being, despite everything. The stone bench warms me from underneath like I'm a lizard. A light breeze keeps me from overheating. The sun plays hide-and-seek behind the clouds, casting an ever-changing pattern of light and shadow over the quad.

Daisy and I are hanging out for a few minutes, after my class and before hers. "I like it," she says of the class, sounding surprised. "I'm making some interesting connections to engineering."

"Really?" I took the same class—and made connections to literature. I suppose we can't ever really disconnect from our majors. They're more than a path of study. They're the lens through which we see the world.

"Like the socio and political factors that influence discovery. We want progress, but science doesn't happen in a vacuum. I'd like to study it more."

As she continues, I can't help but notice a group of students at a nearby table snickering, their eyes darting in our direction. Weird. I give a subtle glance behind me. Nope, no one there. I look down at my clothes, but my jeans and T-shirt don't have any coffee stains.

"What's wrong?" Daisy asks.

I nod to them. "Do I have the imprint of a book on my face or something? I did fall asleep studying last night. I'm so behind on chemistry."

She glances over, frowning. "No, you're fine. They're being assholes."

"Do you know them?"

"No, but I wouldn't mind going over and introducing myself. It would give me a chance to tell them what I think about—"

"Never mind," I say hastily. "Tell me more about the vacuum thing."

We try to go back to our conversation, but the laughter is hard to ignore. It's like a mosquito buzzing around your head—annoying and persistent. Then, two girls saunter by, not even attempting to stifle their giggles as they stare at us.

"Okay," she says. "Are we being hazed?"

I shake my head, feeling a mix of confusion and embarrassment—though I'm not sure what

I'm supposed to be embarrassed about. "I don't know, but we should get going."

She agrees, and we hug before splitting up.

Without the warmth of the stone, the day feels colder. Trees line the path ahead of me like soldiers, their leaves rustling with warning.

A few minutes later, another group of people laugh and point.

Okay, so it was definitely me they're targeting.

What the heck is going on?

The group passes, and that's when I hear it—a snippet of conversation that sends a chill down my spine. "Did you see the latest tea post?" one of them says, followed by a burst of laughter.

My heart skips a beat. Tanglewood Tea.

I duck into the shelter of a building entrance, hands trembling as I pull out my phone. The blood drains from my face as I'm met with Professor Stratford's faculty photo, his stern features twisted into something sinister by a black-and-red filter. The caption reads like a scandal sheet headline: "HOTTEST TEA EVER: Professor Stratford Caught Sleeping with a Student!"

My mind races, replaying every moment I've spent with Stratford in the library, the secluded corners where our passion for Shakespeare—and each other—ignited. Was there a camera? Did I let something slip?

I read the entire post, but it doesn't name me.

Except something made those strangers point and giggle.

I scroll down to the comments.

Students debate Stratford's fate with a mix of moral outrage and lurid fascination. Some demand his dismissal, invoking a morality clause, while others seem more concerned with the professor's undeniable allure.

Then I see it.

The social media app recommends another post, this one referencing the Tanglewood Tea and claiming to work in the administrator's office. They helped create the mentorship schedule for the Tempest Prize, they say.

My name is there, in black and white, for everyone to see.

Anne Hill.

The student most likely to be getting fucked. They can put that under my picture on the yearbook.

The world spins.

My shoulders hit the cold stone of the building. It's out. The secret that could shatter my reputation, my future. Everything.

Do they expel students for that?

Though even if I'm allowed to stay, my name will forever be linked with scandal. Mockery will follow me like a shadow, leaving me cold. If being a woman in academia is hard, being one who fucked a professor will be impossible. The bright future I've envisioned for myself collapses in the span of seconds.

With trembling fingers, I close the app and tuck my phone back into my pocket. I take a deep breath, steeling myself against the whispers and stares that are sure to come. I have to act, to find a way to mitigate the damage, to protect both Stratford and me. But how? I can't even think.

I'm closer to Mayfair than Hathaway. I duck inside the nice dorm, keeping my head down like I'm trying to avoid an unseen threat. Each step feels heavier as I make my way to Carlisle's room.

I knock on the door, half-hoping she's not there. I'm almost too ashamed to face her. She swings the door open. Her eyes go wide with concern. Well, it's clear she's seen the Tanglewood Tea post.

She pulls me inside and shuts the door, her grip firm but gentle.

"Hey," I mumble, not meeting her gaze.

"How are you?" The worry in her voice wraps

around me like a warm blanket, but it only makes me feel more exposed.

My voice trembles. "I don't even know."

She guides me to the couch in her suite, sitting me down and then joining me. A soda appears in my hand. I can't even taste the sweetness. But I feel the bubbly effervescence burn down my throat.

"How did this happen?"

Her dark eyes flash on my behalf. "Some asshole in the admin office who wanted to get views, naming you as if that proves anything. He had no right to do that. And he probably violated an NDA, too."

A random post is not proof.

The fact that he mentored me isn't proof, either.

Then again, they don't need proof. It looks like I'm already indicted by the court of public opinion. And I can't even deny it without lying.

"Everyone already believes it. They were pointing. Laughing."

Carlisle swears under her breath. "Those assholes."

"I'm more mad at Tanglewood Tea than anything," I say, my stomach churning with anger. "They're the ones who started this. The other guy wouldn't have even known what to post if they hadn't called out Stratford."

"Maybe they were trying to help." Her voice is contemplative.

"By humiliating me? By ruining my academic reputation?"

"No, by stopping Professor Stratford. What he's doing isn't right."

I can't help a bitter laugh. "So, you aren't even going to ask if it's true? That I'm the one having an affair with him?"

She shakes her head slowly. "I'm not going to ask."

"Because you already believe it. Like everyone else."

"Listen, if you slept with him, that doesn't reflect on you at all. He's the person in a position of authority. He's the one who took advantage of you."

Even though I understand the argument, even though I might make it if our situations were reversed, something inside me rebels at the idea. It also realizes that this might be really bad for him.

Maybe not in the long term. Men's careers aren't usually penalized for sleeping with young women. But in the short term? Yes.

They might fire him, as the comments suggest.

And it could keep him from exposing the Shakespeare Society.

Is that why they did it?

"Hey, do you think someone paid the Tanglewood Tea to post this? He's been working against this underground society. Maybe if we find out who—"

"I told you last time, there's no breaking through the anonymity. Besides, it doesn't matter. They can't undo it. We need to focus on you right now."

"I'd rather not. It doesn't sound like a great time."

"Listen, I'm going to get my PR person on the phone. She's a big deal. Huge. Like she works for Justin Bieber and Ariana Grande."

"There's no fixing this."

She ignores that and grabs her phone.

I drop back against the couch and bury my face in a pillow as she dials and murmurs to someone on the other end. The reality of everything settles on my chest. I curl up on the couch, my face buried in a pillow.

I'm in the same room but I can't even hear what Carlisle is saying above the dull roar in my head. I can't bring myself to lift my head, to engage with the outside world. It's like I'm trapped in a bubble, the noise of the world around me muffled and distorted.

She returns to me, off the phone now, and takes my hand. "Okay. She says you keep it simple. Don't talk about it. If you're asked about it, don't answer. Or if you really have to, deny it. Say nothing happened."

"But that would be lying."

"Anne. Sweetheart. I love you and your adorable self, but this is not the time for honesty. As long as you don't admit it, you have deniability."

I sigh, not sure I can do it. Not just lie. I'm not sure I can survive being asked. I might just crumble into dust. Actually, that sounds better.

"Though you don't want to lie. The words *no comment* are your best friends right now. Or just say nothing. Like they ask a question? And silence. Or a sidestep. The less you say, the less ammunition they have."

"Maybe I could do the silence thing, since I don't want to talk to any of them. Forever. I'm just going to climb into a hole."

"You're going to get through this. Don't confirm anything, not to friends, not to the press, and for the love of God, not to the university administration."

My heart thuds. "You think they're going to question me?"

"Maybe. It depends on how Stratford plays this."

I shiver at the idea of being questioned by Dean Morris. I have a thing about authority, especially in academic places.

I'm not sure I can lie to him.

"What if Stratford sues the Tanglewood Tea? He can find out their source. Or at least get them to take their post down."

"He could try, but it's tricky. It's only libel if it's true. And the source might be covered under the freedom of press."

Frustration makes my cheeks warm. "They're not the freaking *New York Times*. Most of what they post is who's dating who."

Her voice turns gentle. "The damage is probably already done."

"You're right." I drop my head, unable to hold it up. "They could take down the post right now, and everyone would still believe it. Maybe it would even prove it to some of the skeptics."

She pulls me into a tight hug. "I believe in you."

"I don't know what I would do without you."

"You're not alone in this. We'll get through it,

okay?"

I nod against her shoulder, grateful for her support. And her expert knowledge of PR, something I've never dealt with. I never imagined it would even be part of my life. Now I'm caught in a whirlwind of scandal, my future hanging by a thread.

# CHAPTER TWENTY-TWO

Shakespeare Fangirl

I KEEP MY head bowed as I cross the campus, not wanting to be recognized.

Now I understand why Carlisle spends so much time in her suite. The little box in Hathaway is my only refuge. I would have gone straight there after leaving Mayfair, except for the curt email from Professor Thorne telling me to meet in her office.

Nothing good will happen there, that's for sure.

I've gotten some texts from Daisy, who has no doubt heard the news. I can't talk to her now, because I'd have a complete breakdown. And I'd like the relative comfort of my lumpy bed to do that.

I'm so focused on trying to become one with the pavement that I nearly collide with a solid form. My heart leaps into my throat before I manage a muttered, "Sorry," and move to sidestep the obstacle. But then I look up.

Brandon is there, his expression hurt before it hardens into an icy mask. "My mom told me girls love guys who're into Shakespeare, but I thought she was bullshitting. Apparently not."

"It's not what it sounds like."

"That's why you were with me, wasn't it? To get close to my father."

"What?"

"You were willing to fuck both of us to get what you wanted."

My stomach twists. "I understand why you're upset, but it wasn't like that. I didn't even know Professor Stratford was going to be teaching here until after…"

Until after I had sex with him for money at a hotel.

Somehow I don't think that will soothe Brandon's anger.

He laughs, a bitter sound that feels wrong from someone his age. "Sure, and I'm supposed to believe you, a freaking Shakespeare fangirl, had no idea who he was?"

"I swear I didn't—"

His eyes rake over me with contempt. "You're pathetic."

His words are like a slap across the face. I feel my cheeks burn with humiliation and a surge of anger. "You don't get to talk to me like that."

"What are you going to do about it? Run and tell my dad?"

Before I can respond, he stalks off, leaving me standing there, exposed and vulnerable. There are whispers. A confrontation isn't exactly the best way to stay anonymous. I look up just in time to see a student pointing their phone at me. The flash goes off, capturing my misery for the world to see.

Another post for Tanglewood Tea, maybe.

They haven't yet posted that I'm the one who had sex with Professor Stratford, which is strange since it would be extremely hot gossip. No one picked up on the fact that I dated Stratford's son…until now.

Tanglewood Tea would have already known, though, since they reported on him cheating on me last summer. That's why we even broke up. Maybe they weren't able to confirm that it was me? Or maybe they do know, but they think I'm the victim like Carlisle does, so it's some kind of journalistic integrity about it. If that's the case, it's a little too late.

I continue on my way to Professor Thorne's

office, ignoring the stares.

The door to her office is ajar when I arrive, and I can see her sitting behind her desk. I knock, and she looks up, her cold gaze assessing me.

"Have a seat, Ms. Hill." Her voice is cold, devoid of any sympathy.

I obey her, wondering if she's going to question me. If I'm going to have to say *no comment.* So far, I've gotten no summons from Dean Morris.

I take the chair opposite her desk, my hands clasped tightly.

Professor Thorne leans back in her chair, a self-satisfied smile playing on her lips. "It seems your academic career has taken a bit of a tumble, hasn't it?"

I'm taken aback by her bluntness, but I struggle to hide it. If she wants to get a rise out of me, she'll have to do better than that. "What do you mean?"

She raises an eyebrow, clearly not buying my act. "Don't play coy with me. The entire university is buzzing with the news of your little affair. Is that what people are calling it these days? I feel like that implies some emotion, but I think you and I both know it wasn't about that. It wasn't even about sex. No, it was a transaction."

My cheeks flush. She's closer to the mark than she thinks, considering how Stratford and I met. I keep my voice even, though. "Is there a reason you asked for this meeting?"

"Oh, yes. I wanted to be the one to tell you the sad news…for supportive reasons, of course. As your professor this semester, I'm so very sorry to inform you that your entry for the Tempest Prize has been disqualified."

My breath catches. "Why?"

She leans forward on her elbows. "The board of the award was shocked to learn that you were sleeping with your mentor."

Anger makes my fists clench at my sides. "Even if I did it, which I'm not saying I did, why would that impact my entry?"

"You slept with Stratford in order to get him to write your paper."

I stare at her in disbelief. "What? That's not what happened."

She snorts. "I read your entry. Your arguments were far too sophisticated for an undergraduate. It's clear he wrote it for you. Mentors are allowed to provide advice and support…up to a point. Not create the entire argument from scratch."

There's an irony here. It's almost a compliment that Thorne believes my paper was too good to have been written by me. Because the fact is, I did write it. From the original concept all the way to the final draft, it was mine.

There's no way to prove it, however.

It occurs to me that sometimes people accuse others of their own sins. "I wrote my paper," I say. "Which is more than I can say for Matteo."

A dismissive wave of her hand. "Don't try to turn this around."

"It's not hard to guess that you were going to choose Matteo to mentor regardless of what we'd written that day in class."

Her expression hardens, and for a moment, I see a flicker of guilt cross her features. Then she laughs, a harsh, bitter sound that fills the room. "Matteo was always going to win that prize. You never had a chance."

It's basically an admission.

One that doesn't help me at all.

"So he won?"

"They haven't announced the winners yet, but as his mentor I was told privately to clear my calendar for the award ceremony. It will look nice on my wall, don't you think?"

Her walls have almost no room for new accolades. They had seemed impressive when I first met her, but now I have to wonder how many were earned on merit—and how many she manipulated.

"You cheated," I whisper, knowing she's the one who called the board. The one who claimed I hadn't written my paper.

"And you lost." Her voice is flat, her eyes almost reptilian.

"That's your problem. You think someone else has to lose for you to win."

"That's how the prize works. More importantly, that's how the world works. I think you've found that out the hard way, Ms. Hill."

She's right about one thing. I've lost. More than my reputation, I've lost the bright-eyed innocence that Carlisle found so adorable. "I may have lost the Tempest Prize, but at least I still have my integrity."

I leave, both defeated and reaffirmed.

Because she's wrong about the most important thing.

This isn't a zero-sum game. It's not a resource we need to hoard.

Knowledge is the one thing that we can share without diminishing ourselves. That may seem simple, but that doesn't mean it's not true. And I'll float down the river, my skirts wide like

Ophelia, singing that song even as I drown, even as she watches me sink.

I'm basically numb as I make my way back to the dorm room.

Lying on my thin mattress in the dorm room, I stare at the ceiling, finding gruesome scenes in the clumpy, yellowed popcorn texture.

My hands fold on my stomach.

I look like Ophelia in her death scene—if I were wearing a gorgeous, flowing dress instead of jeans and a T-shirt, if I were holding a sheaf of flowers instead of my phone, if I were a tragic beauty instead of a ruined co-ed.

It's all very melodramatic in my head, but those are the perils of reading that much Shakespeare. My mind is a whirlwind of betrayal, disappointment, and a future that seems to be crumbling before my eyes.

I don't know how much time has passed before the door creaks.

Daisy walks in, her arms laden with bags. "I hate every single one of those fuckers. But don't worry, I brought reinforcements." She dumps a brown paper bag upside down on her bed. "Super cheap alcohol that's one step above Windex, a THC gummy, and something even harder if you want a real trip."

They don't tempt me.

The weird thing about the pain is that I want to feel it. I want to wallow in it, let it consume me. It's a twisted comfort, a reminder that I'm still alive, still capable of feeling something, even if it's misery.

Daisy sits down on the edge of my bed. "What the actual fuck?"

The harshness of the words isn't directed at me. It's at the world. If she had come to me with sympathy or pity, I would have had to reject it. The hard words allow me to speak, to tell her about Brandon's confrontation and Carlisle's PR plan. And the most painful part: losing the Tempest Prize.

She fumes for me. "I'm literally going to kill someone. Probably this Professor Thorne lady. But also Brandon. That little fucker cheated on you, and he called you a slut?"

I think that cluster of popcorn ceiling looks like a skull, like the symbol of the Society. I can't believe I never noticed that before. "It doesn't matter."

"It matters because it's an antiquated sexist slur. And because it's not even true. You've literally had sex with one person."

"Which is now public knowledge."

"And fuck the prize. You're the smartest person I know."

"You programmed a robot dog to fetch."

She rolls her beautiful blue eyes. "Yeah, I can make wires and code. Big deal. You're going to change the world, Anne. I knew it as soon as I met you."

A snort.

"I'm serious. This Tempest Prize can go to hell. For them to believe Thorne, as if she's possibly unbiased when she's competing against you. They don't deserve to publish your piece."

"Yes, I'm sure it's a great loss to the academic community."

"You're going to win a Nobel Prize someday, and when you do, you could call out people like Thorne, but you're going to do something even better. You're going to have forgotten about her completely. But she'll still think about you until she dies, feeling jealous, fading away, turning into an old crone who lures small children with candy before eating them alive."

"That got dark."

"I got a little carried away, but you know what? I stand by it."

I can't even feel pleasure at the fantasy future.

There's a knock on the dorm room.

Our residential advisor, Lorelei, steps inside. She's usually strict about the rules. And not exactly gentle about it. I'm half expecting her to tell me that I'm being expelled from the dorm, kicked out for being a super slut.

Her brown eyes are surprisingly soft. "This note came for you."

Our mail usually gets put in the cubbies for us to take out. Not exactly secure but then again no one is sending anyone in Hathaway large chunks of cash or anything people would want to steal.

I have no idea why she's hand-delivering this.

Though I can't bring myself to care.

Daisy's the one who takes the note with a thanks. They murmur at the door about who-knows-what before she returns to me. "Do you want me to open it?"

"Whatever."

There's tearing. "It's from Stratford."

I blink, trying not to care.

"At least, I assume that's who it's from. It's signed W.S. You don't know William Shatner, do you? I mean you may not know him from that small gig he did in *Star Trek*, but he was a trained Shakespearean actor."

My lips curl into a smile despite my best efforts.

She cheers for herself, making the sound of a

touchdown or some other ballgame that I don't understand. "You know, I just realized he has the same initials as Shakespeare. Do you think he was destined to study him?"

I sit up and accept the note.

We need to talk. The usual place. Room 516.

There's also a hotel key card. It doesn't say the Pinnacle on it. Instead there's an art deco design of emerald and gold geometric lines.

"Anne," she says softly, her hand reaching out to still mine as I clutch the note tightly. "You don't have to go. You can ignore it. You get to choose."

I nod, knowing she's right.

Except this is my choice.

He is my choice.

I want to know whether he's okay, how he's faring in the scandal. I even want to know if there's some way I can help, unlikely as that seems. Love is deep water. We put the chains on ourselves. And God help me, I want the weight of them. I've fallen for my professor. I love William Stratford. There's no triumph in it. No relief. Only the awareness of a long way down in inky depths.

CHAPTER TWENTY-THREE

Six-Letter Word

THE PINNACLE HOTEL feels like stepping into another world where the air is perfumed with wealth and power. The chandeliers cast a warm, golden glow over the opulent lobby. Plush velvet chaises invite the elite to sink into luxury.

Twice now Stratford has been my unexpected savior here.

Now what is he? I'm not sure.

I make my way to the brass elevator and go up beside a gorgeous blonde woman who's dressed in a trench coat and heels. Definitely seems like she's heading to a room for sex, but is it an illicit affair? A call girl thing? Or maybe a married couple on a date, the kids at home with the babysitter.

Though the more prescient question is what I'm heading to the room for. Sex? Likely. Our chemistry seems irrepressible. Love? Unlikely, at least on his end. I believe he has some tenderness for me, some affection, but that has nothing to do with deep waters. A man like him is never going to drown.

At least not over little Annie Hill.

Most likely this meeting is a strategy session. For all I know, he might even have PR people who want to coach me on what not to say. Or a lawyer who has a confidentiality agreement for me to sign. *I hereby swear that I will never tell anyone that I sucked William Stratford's cock, that I loved doing it, that I imagine about the taste when I touch myself, that I almost need it to orgasm.*

The elevator dings. I step into the hushed corridor of the fifth floor.

Maybe he called me here to punish me for the scandal with rough sex. If that's the case, I'll take the sting, the burn, the lash of his dominance. It might not take away his frustration, but I think it might somehow soothe mine.

The key card turns the little light green.

With a resolute push, I open the door and step inside.

The walls are a deep teal. They catch the light from the vintage brass sconces. A silver tray with a decanter of amber liquid and two crystal glasses rests on the small table beside it. The carpet beneath my heels is plush, a symphony of swirling patterns in shades of cream and gold that makes me feel like I'm walking on a cloud.

Floor-to-ceiling windows reveal the glittering skyline of Tanglewood City.

Though the view that takes my breath away is Stratford.

He's dressed in a crisp white shirt, the top few buttons undone to reveal a tantalizing glimpse of tanned skin. His sleeves are rolled up to his elbows, showcasing muscular forearms. Even from the other side of the suite, the air is filled with the faint scent of sandalwood and something else, something uniquely him. It's a high beyond any gummy or pill that Daisy could find.

"Anne." A storm brews in his gaze—regret, desire, a hint of something I can't quite place. Lights cast long shadows across his chiseled features.

The door falls shut behind me with that heavy way of hotel doors.

"Professor Stratford," I reply, my voice steadier than I feel.

"I'm sorry."

The simple words destroy my defenses. "For what? You weren't the one who published the post on Tanglewood Tea, were you?"

He moves around the room, not approaching

me. "No, but I was the one who arranged to mentor you. I was the one who had sex with you at all, which meant that there was anything to discover."

I find myself moving counter to him, letting the fashionable furniture stand between us, not sure what will happen when we collide. "I think the worst thing you probably did to me was take on the Society. They're probably the source that tipped off whoever runs the account."

"Probably."

"Though…" I stand still, allowing him to catch me. "If you hadn't taken on the Society, you wouldn't have come back to Tanglewood. You wouldn't have been my professor. You wouldn't have found me here last semester."

Expressions move across his face like quicksilver. A lamp hangs down like an upside-down triangle, its pearl-white panels held in place by gold metal. It highlights them like a movie strip: possessiveness, grief. "Someone else would have touched you. Some other bastard would have taken your virginity. It didn't even happen, and I want to find the imaginary fucker and kill him." He pauses. "Which sounds fucked up when I say it out loud."

"You're a little unhinged. Then again, so am

I."

Another step, and he's standing in front of me, his expression severe, his sandalwood scent enveloping me. He looks like he wants to devour me. But he doesn't. Because of the rumors? He might not have called me here for sex or strategy.

He might have called me here to say goodbye.

"Hi," I say.

His lips curve. "Hi."

"I don't suppose anything interesting has happened lately?"

"Nah, I've had to resort to finishing crossword puzzles to fill the time."

I grin. "What's a six-letter word for catastrophe?"

"Fiasco."

Even though we're talking about something serious, it feels like flirting. This is the same game we played on the first night, when he asked for six-letter words to describe my body. *Chubby*, I said. *Erotic*, he said.

Though the word of the night was *virgin*.

As in, I sold it to him.

"Turkey," I say, adding to the list.

He snorts. "Foul-up."

"That's two words."

"Not according to the Oxford English Dictionary."

God. Why was a smart man so freaking hot to me? "Defeat."

He shakes his head slowly. "We're not defeated."

"You sound a little defeated if you don't have another word."

"Upturn."

"Anything is an upturn when you're at rock bottom."

"Exactly, Ms. Hill." He sounded so much like he did in the lecture hall, a kind of condescension with a low, intimate rumble that makes me so freaking aroused. I sway, and he catches me in his arms. His expression is knowing, because of course it is. The freaking intelligence. So annoying.

"How bad has it been?" I ask.

"That's what I want to ask you."

"Well, I said it first."

"It's been…bad. The calls. The bullshit with the school. The worst part is Brandon. He's pissed as hell, and I can't really blame him."

"He was mad at me, too."

His eyes narrow. "He called you? What did he say?"

"No, he ran into me on campus. He was upset. I think we were both in shock."

"He shouldn't have done that. You've done nothing wrong."

"It feels good to hear you say that, considering the number of derisive looks I've gotten in the past few days, but I'm not sure I totally agree."

He looks genuinely annoyed. "You needed money for textbooks for college. Then you ended up my student, under my influence. I don't see how that means you did anything wrong. If anything, it proves that the academic system is a fucking caste system parading as a meritocracy."

I can't hold back a smile.

"What?" he asks.

"I've just never really seen you mad before. I mean you've been like stern and controlling and you were even an asshole at the Provost's house that night, but I've never seen you…you know, worked up. It's kinda hot."

His expression softens. "Your turn. How bad has it been?"

I tell him about the Tempest Prize, which has become basically old news at this point. Based on his little rant about the faux meritocracy, I expect him to erupt. I also expect it will be hot. Unfortunately, he turns unnaturally still.

And pulls out his phone.

"Umm, who are you calling?"

"I won't let this happen."

"Listen, I don't know if you have the board people on speed dial, but I don't think they're going to react well if you are the one disputing the claim. Besides, it's already done. They're already having the plaque, or whatever it is, printed with Matteo's name on it."

"I don't know the board. I know who *funds* the board, which is even better. He's an old drama nerd who gives loads of money to Shakespearean causes when he's not hanging out with his vintage cars or his pet falcon."

"You know him?"

"He was on this science fiction show. We met when I was doing consulting for this King Lear episode."

"Wait. Is it William Shatner?"

"No."

"More than one of them love Shakespeare?"

"When I'm done with them, there's not even going to be a Tempest Prize."

"Wait." I put a hand on his cellphone and lower it. "Don't."

"They're going to regret this."

"Maybe, but I don't want it to be because we ended the prize. Even if they basically stole it this time around, that doesn't mean it's broken every year."

"Fuck."

"Those other people deserve to win."

"How can you be calm about this?"

"I'm not happy about it, but I'm also…used to it."

"Used to losing the Tempest Prize?"

"Used to the world being unfair. I mean, it sucks. I'm pretty mad, actually. I think later I'll have to cry about it. But the important thing is, it doesn't stop me. It hasn't stopped me. Even not getting textbook money didn't stop me. That's what this hotel represents. I am determined to make this happen, so this can't stop me. Simple as that."

"I'm in awe of you."

"You wrote a literal book on Shakespeare."

"Yes, with the privilege of being male, raised on Shakespeare from the time I can remember speaking. My father sang 'How Should I Your True Love Know?' instead of nursery rhymes."

"Is that a real thing that happened or are you joking? Sometimes I can't tell."

"The point is, the Tempest Prize could change someone's life. But it wasn't going to change yours. Because it's like you said. Nothing is going to stop you."

"Aww, that's kind of sweet as a compliment. Also kind of sad. I mean, I'll do it anyway, but I wouldn't have *minded* a life-changing award."

"You're going to win a hundred of them. A thousand. You're going to do it the same way you deserved to win this one, by caring more about the paper than about the award money."

"You're actually kind of sweet when you aren't pretending to be a megalomaniac society person."

"Was it the cape?"

"It was. Yes."

He grins at me. "You're going to have to accept my money."

"What?"

"I can't keep bribing the bartenders here."

"So that's how you knew I was here."

"He also watered down your drinks."

"But I paid full price."

"Actually, you didn't pay for them at all."

"Oh my God. Did we leave without paying? Because that's very like down-with-the-one-percent, social justice of me. Except I should have tipped the bartender, even if I wasn't going to pay the bill. We should probably tell them."

"I paid the tab before I even got there."

"That's a relief."

He smiles. "You're charming."

"Is that code for—"

For being innocent. I don't get to finish the words, because he's kissing me. There's a faint flavor of whiskey mixing with something essential, the essence of William Stratford. He kisses me like we have nowhere to go, nothing to do except explore new angles to rub against each other. My nerves come alight.

His hands are sure, confident. They skim down my neck, down the sides of my breasts. He lifts my T-shirt away. My breath unhitches as he see me bare, wearing only a plain cotton bra and jeans. I realize now how much the dresses, the makeup, the shoes—they're armor. And wearing my regular clothes, I'm worse than naked. Completely vulnerable.

I move to cover myself, but he grasps my wrists, turning me so that I'm facing away. Facing the city. Something silky soft wraps around my wrist. His tie, I realize. My breath catches, and I struggle. "What are you doing?"

"Well," he murmurs. "You see, I'm pretty angry about something I heard recently. Someone fucked over the woman I love."

"The woman you—"

"And I wasn't allowed to ruin their lives."

"Did you say that you—"

"I'm afraid I'll have to take out all my frustration on your sweet little body." He turns me around to face him. "Yes, dear heart. Did you not know? You know everything except how irresistible you are."

I'm not sure what to feel about such a direct compliment.

But I don't have to decide, because I'm immediately thrown into an entirely deeper quandary when he says, "I love you."

"You do?"

"And now I'm going to fuck you."

"I love you, too."

He pauses only briefly at the words, continuing to bend me gently but firmly over the curved arm of the velvet sofa. Then my jeans are pulled down unceremoniously, along with my panties. Only my bra is left, but as I look down to where my breasts are hanging, the cleavage made sharp by the heavy swing, the cotton almost looks like fancy lingerie.

His lips scorch a path down my spine. He nips at my skin before laving the spot with his tongue. The trail of sensation leaves fire in its wake. I squirm, but I can't escape the exquisite torment.

Finally, his mouth finds my cunt, and I can't hold back the moan that escapes my lips. His tongue circles my clit, teasing me, tormenting me. This is the punishment he meant, and I'm begging. To stop. To never, ever stop.

He alternates between soft, gentle licks and firmer, more insistent strokes, driving me wild with desire. I'm panting, my body trembling on the edge of release. "Do you know," he says, his voice almost casual, only the barest hint of tension, "I don't believe I ever paid you back for that blowjob."

The one where I edged him over and over again until he was shaking.

He pulls back, leaving me aching and empty, and I can't help but whimper at the loss of contact. A dark chuckle fills me with an intense yearning. I want him to touch me, but I know it only ends with me empty, throbbing, wanting.

This will be a long, beautiful night of retribution.

CHAPTER TWENTY-FOUR

My Own Merits

I'M ON THE sixth floor again.

It's not one of the scheduled mentorship sessions. In fact, Stratford isn't even here. I'm alone getting in some studying time before finals.

It's been two nights since the Pinnacle.

Before we left, Stratford told me he's quitting. Which alarmed me, but he's sure it will help. For one thing, it would shut down the rumors involving me as much as possible.

It would also imply guilt on his part, improving my reputation.

Absolutely not, I told him.

Until he explained that he had a pile of money sitting around in his bank account and also a network that would be happy to work with him in a year.

Most important of all, it would get the Society to back off.

He isn't going to walk away, but it would be good if they thought so.

I try to focus again on the chemistry report in front of me, but really, my God. Letters aren't supposed to look like this.

The elevator slides open, which is a little surprising. No one ever comes here. Soft footfalls. A shadow flickers at the edge of my vision.

Carlisle peeks around the tall bookshelves lined with dusty old tomes. Curly brown hair spills over her shoulders, framing her face. Even with minimal makeup and an oversized hoodie designed for paparazzi sightings, she still transforms the place into the set of a hip music video.

"There you are," she says.

I glance over my shoulder. "What are you doing here?"

"Looking for you." She grimaces. "I had to reach out to that guy who outed you to find out where your mentorship sessions were held."

My pulse picks up. "What's wrong?"

"There's a rumor."

"Do not even say the words Tanglewood Tea."

"It's not on there. This is…worse."

"What is it?"

"There's something big happening in the

humanities department right now. People are saying it's a coup, like an academic bloodbath."

My blood runs cold. "What does this have to do with me?"

"I don't know. Maybe nothing. Except that Stratford is involved. And with the connection to you, I just had to see for myself that you were okay."

"What do you mean, involved? Like he's taking over."

"No, he's being overthrown."

The world around me seems to tilt on its axis. "I'll go to him."

"That's the thing. He's gone."

Gone? "This is kind of a secret, but Stratford was quitting. So maybe he's just not in his office because he turned in his resignation."

She looks worried. Not about him. About me.

"You saw him again, didn't you?"

I'm surprised by the feeling that I need to defend myself. Carlisle has always been open-minded, though now that I think about it, she was pretty hard on Stratford when the news came out. A lot of people were.

"Look, I know it sounds crazy, and this isn't the time, really, if some bad stuff is happening, but I love him. And he loves me."

Her mouth falls into an *O*. "Anne."

Anne, she says, as if I'm an idiot. And maybe I am. Did he turn in his resignation and then…leave campus? He told me to wait, to trust him, to let him quit, and then we'd figure out a way to be together until I graduated. Except what if that's all bullshit you tell an inconvenient prostitute-slash-undergrad?

No, I'm overreacting. It's just Carlisle's worry.

And something else.

A strange energy that becomes more apparent as I emerge from the library. It's as if the campus has been pressed into a socket, an undercurrent of tension that makes everyone walk a little faster, their heads down.

It's the animals in us. They know something dangerous is happening.

I reach Professor Stratford's office on campus. I haven't been here all semester, but it's exactly where I remember it. The door is ajar.

Cold dread settles over me.

He's someone who usually has stacks of papers and folders and notebooks. Now, there's a credit card on the floor by his desk. No, not a credit card. It's the room key. The same one he gave me, with the emerald-and-gold pattern.

I turn it over, check underneath. Nothing.

Is this supposed to be a message? Or is this a piece of trash he tossed on his way out? Probably trash, but as usual I really can't tell. I hope he hasn't done something spy-worthy like encode a secret message on the little door-opening part, because I don't have time to get Daisy.

There's one person who will know what happened, whether Stratford quit or not, where he is right now. My heart is pounding as I cross the campus. First I'm fast-walking, then flat-out sprinting.

There's the familiar gold placard, the oak door.

Except when I open it, the office looks completely different.

I pick up the letter, my hands trembling as I read the words that confirm my worst fears. It's a typed resignation letter thanking the university for his years here, saying he had to retire suddenly for personal reasons. A generic-sounding letter. I wouldn't even know it was from him if he hadn't signed the bottom.

My heart sinks.

Somehow, they've gotten rid of him.

Probably because he was getting too close to the truth. The Shakespeare Society struck back, and like all dying things, they struck back hard.

Luca Andini saunters in. My blood runs cold as he closes the door behind him, his dark eyes lingering on me with a predatory intensity.

The letter flutters from my hand. "What are you doing here?"

Green eyes glint with amusement. "This is my office now. Since Dean Morris left his post so...suddenly, I'm helping my alma mater by stepping in as temporary dean."

The room tilts, the walls closing in as the gravity of his words sinks in. "Dean Morris would never leave like this," I say, my anger a welcome shield against the fear. "You've done something to him—"

A dismissive wave of his hand. "Perhaps he simply wanted to spend more time with his lovely family. Before something terrible happened to them."

A chill runs down my spine. The framed photograph on Morris's desk, the one of him with his arm around a gorgeous dark-haired woman, a little girl with pigtails perched on his shoulders, is gone. The image of their smiling faces is a stark contrast to the hard lines of Luca's cruel grin.

Morris, with his military bearing and the jagged scar that marred his cheek, wasn't a man who scared easily. He'd faced down enemies in combat, fought for his country, and carried the weight of those experiences with a quiet strength that commanded respect. But this wasn't about him anymore. It was about the people he loved, the family he would do anything to protect. How could he stand against an enemy that targeted those he held most dear?

"You won't get away with this."

"You of all people know what I'm capable of."

The air between us crackles with tension, a silent battle of wills. Even as we both know that I'm outmatched. Luca has more power in his little finger than I've ever had.

"Oh, where is that boyfriend of yours? Not around to protect you anymore?"

I turn cold. And then hot all over. "What did you do to him?"

"Anything I want. That's the point. This is only one piece. The Society controls every part of the city."

I retreat to the relative safety of the door, a public space that would make dismemberment a little tricky, even for someone this bold. I lock eyes with Luca, my gaze a challenge to his arrogance. "Almost every part, but you missed something. Because you sure as hell don't control me."

I'm not a fighter, not physically, anyway. My weapons are words. And I show up to the Mayfair armed and dangerous. I knock on his door at the Mayfair.

The dorm features privacy as a perk, with celebrities like Carlisle, with children of senators or foreign royalty. Or in this case, with wealthy sons of megalomaniacs. But their rooms are an open secret.

His eyes narrow when he opens the door. "You."

"Here's the deal," I say, sweeping inside. His suite is even larger than Carlisle's, which is wild. I didn't even know you could upgrade. Apparently she'd gone low-key with her nine-hundred-square-foot suite. "I need information. And I need it fast."

"Why the fuck would I help you?"

"Because you're gay. And while I don't care about that, your father does."

He lifts his top lip in a beautiful sneer. "It's the twenty-first century. What gave you that idea?"

"Oh, for starters, the fact that he's living in the sixteenth century," I say, ticking them off on my fingers. "Then there's the fact that he offered to share me with everyone there, including you.

And lastly because you lashed out like a wild animal when I happened to see you kissing a guy."

His expression hardens. "Fuck off."

"So here's the deal: you're going to help me find Stratford or I'm going to Luca Andini, sorry, I mean, *Dean* Luca Andini, and telling him about you."

"You're a bitch."

A brief smile touches my lips. It's not the first time I've been called that. In a twisted way, my father trained me to take the kind of bullshit women get in the workplace. "Am I a bitch or am I just not taking your family's bullshit?"

"I don't know where Stratford is."

"Then find out."

A few minutes later we have our answer. He's in one of the old underground nuclear shelters, the ones the society controls. I attended a party there at my first event. Matteo also produces a key.

His stony expression makes it clear he doesn't enjoy being blackmailed. Which is understandable. Though maybe he should try less evil hijinks.

"Don't tell him I'm heading there," I say. "Or the deal's off."

He shakes his head. "For what it's worth, I didn't want the Tempest Prize that way. I wanted to win it on my own merits."

I don't know whether he means with the initial boost of Thorne's mentorship, which probably included her writing the paper. Or whether he means the way I was kicked out. "Funny, so did I."

It's raining by the time I exit the dorm, the sky a tumultuous canvas of London-fog grays and deep purples. The students around me huddle under umbrellas and hoods, their conversations a low murmur that weaves through the patter of raindrops on the pavement. I pass a group gathered beneath the awning of the student center, their words carrying over the din of the storm.

I catch a few words that tell me they're talking about the humanities department. "A real Shakespearean tragedy," one of them says, sounding amused at their own joke. "Like, the power struggles, the backstabbing."

"The ruthless takeover of it all."

The casual banter feels like acid on an open wound.

I can't help but bristle at their casual dismissal of the situation. They're acting like it's some Netflix show they've binged. They don't know how dangerous the Society is, or even that the coup is run by them.

They don't know what's at stake, which will make fighting this harder.

That's a problem for another day, though.

Right now, I need to find Stratford.

I pause beneath the shelter of a large oak tree, its branches providing a meager respite from the relentless downpour. My trembling fingers move over the screen of my phone as I write a quick email to Professor Avery Miller, explaining what I know and exactly where I'm going. She's one of the few people on campus I can trust right now, but I don't know when she'll get this. I'm not even sure she's still a professor here.

Another email I send to Cormac Stratford, William's brother. I've never even spoken to him before, so I have no idea whether he'll believe me. It might come across as the new junk spam. Instead of sending money to a Nigerian prince, it's getting your brother out of the clutches of a secret society.

I hope they can help, because I don't have much faith in my own ability to get Stratford out of this. But I can't sit around while he might be hurt.

A chill runs down my spine, and it's not just from the cold rain soaking through my clothes.

The thought of what might have already been done to him sends waves of nausea and panic through me. Would they have hit him? Probably. It's crude, but Andini is really just a brunt-force bully beneath the Society's ritualistic robes.

Stratford will still be alive, though.

I have to believe that.

Even if Andini were willing to murder, an idea that doesn't exactly stretch the imagination, he would keep Stratford alive if only to gloat. At least, I hope so. The alternative is too hard to even consider.

My brain swerves away from the despair waiting there.

I'm fully drenched by the time I reach the half-hidden door, a slab of inconspicuous metal that looks like it leads to some utility room. I use the code Matteo gave me on the keypad. It unlatches.

The air grows cooler as I make my way down the steps, the only sound the echo of my own footsteps reverberating off the concrete walls. The underground nuclear shelter, a relic of a bygone era, has been repurposed by the Shakespeare Society for their parties. For free drugs and orgies.

The front porch, Andini called them.

There's no party happening now. It's dark and

dim.

I want to call out for him, but something tells me to stay quiet.

I'm not alone down here.

The cold air in the underground shelter makes goose bumps rise on my skin. Or maybe it's the eerie silence. The only sound is the soft brush of my shoes against concrete. I dial 9-1-1, turn the volume way down, and leave my phone on the floor, facedown in the shadows.

Whatever happens now, at least they'll know where I went.

I find a trail of footprints in the dust.

There's a dark patch on the ground. Blood.

My fingers brush against the cool wall to guide me. Out of nowhere, I'm yanked backward, my body slammed against a wall. A knife glints in the dim light, the blade pressed against my throat.

Fear lances through me, sharp and icy. I can't breathe, can't think. Terror even blinds me for a moment, before I recognize Stratford. He looks wholly changed. More animalistic. A different creature than the one at Pinnacle.

He sucks in a breath. The knife is gone. "What are you doing here?"

He's disheveled, his dark hair falling over his forehead, a wildness in his eyes I've never seen before. There's a dark stain on his shirt, spreading across his side. Blood. "Oh, you know, I came to ask you out. Watch a movie. Grab some fro-yo. Typical date things."

"You need to get the fuck out of here," he growls.

"I'm not leaving you," I say, my voice steadier than I feel. My hands flutter to his wound, and he winces. "We're going to get you to a hospital."

He pants, leaning back against the wall now that he's not busy trying to attack someone. "It's too late for that."

My heart pounds. "What do you mean?"

"They got me through Brandon."

"He did this to you?"

"No, but that might have been easier to accept. My ex used him to get me down here. They were waiting for me."

"Why would she do that?"

His teeth gleam white as he gives a pained laugh. "She's offended that I fucked someone, ironically. That's what brought me down. Simple jealousy, even though we haven't shared a bed or a civil word in decades."

"An ambulance is coming. I already called them."

"They poisoned the blade, Anne. I managed

to get two of them, and they took off, but it was too late. They'd already done it."

Fear, visceral and white-hot, burns through me. "This is insane."

"There is nothing good or bad but thinking makes it so."

"I can't believe I'm saying this, but now is *not* the time for Shakespeare."

"I knew the risks when I came back. I'm only sorry that I dragged you into this. The important thing is that you go. Not the dorm. Not home. Go far away. Secret. Safe. Cormac can help."

"Don't you dare pass out on me," I say, my voice breaking.

I'm not worried about him passing out. I'm worried about him dying.

That this breath might be his last. Or this one. Or this.

He slides down the concrete wall. His eyes flutter open, a look of surprise on his face. "I didn't expect...to fall in love with you," he murmurs, his voice barely a whisper. "But I did. It's the best thing I've ever done."

I press my hand to his wound, applying pressure in a desperate attempt to slow the bleeding. Except I might make it worse. I don't know how you treat poison. "We're going to get through this," I say, as if I can make it true. Tears blur my vision. "You're going to be okay."

A soft sigh escaping his lips.

"No," I say, my voice rising in panic. "Don't you dare leave me, William. Don't you dare. I will bring you back from the dead and kill you."

His eyes close. He's limp in my arms. I cradle him against me, rocking back and forth as soundless sobs wrack my body. I came here to save him, and instead, I watched him die.

Thank you for reading THE STUDENT!

Find out who comes down the basement steps. Does William ever wake up? Does Anne escape the Society? THE FINAL EXAM is the breathtaking conclusion to the trilogy.

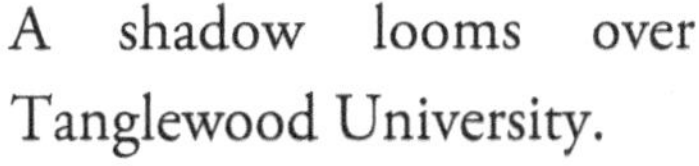
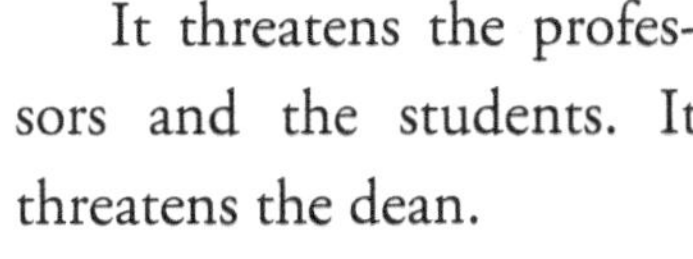
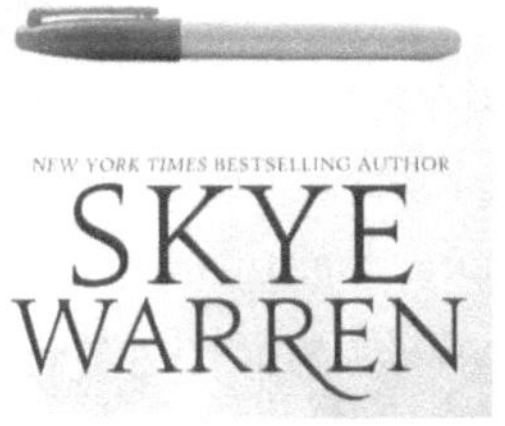

A shadow looms over Tanglewood University.

It threatens the professors and the students. It threatens the dean.

I'm powerless to stop corruption that goes deep into the city's underworld.

Professor William Stratford has the secrets we need. And I find inside me a strength that has nothing to do with escaping my family. It has to do with building a new one.

We need more than bravery to win, but it will mean nothing without love.

Get THE FINAL EXAM now!

Want to read Dean Morris's story? His steamy duet is out now!

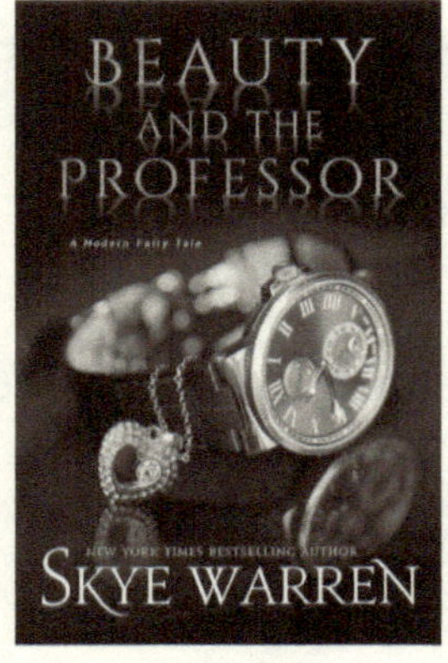

Once upon a time there was a beautiful college student…

Erin cleans Mr. Morris's house twice a week to pay her tuition. The reclusive ex-soldier intimidates her, but she can't help but feel sympathy for him. Then she walks in on him touching himself, and she has much darker, much more sensual feelings.

And a beastly professor with scars he can't hide…

Blake Morris knows he's scarred both inside and out. He's reclusive and surly. Nowhere near good enough for the smart and beautiful young woman who cleans his house.

He receives an offer to return to his alma mater as an associate professor. This is his chance to reenter the world—and to be worthy of the woman he dreams about. He never expected to see her sitting in his classroom on the first day of the semester.

Get BEAUTY AND THE PROFESSOR now!

Sign up for the VIP Reader List to get free books, bonus scenes, and find out when my books go on sale:

https://www.skyewarren.com/newsletter

I appreciate your help in spreading the word, including telling a friend. Reviews help readers find books! Please leave a review on your favorite book site.

You can also join my Facebook group, Skye Warren's Dark Room, for exclusive giveaways and sneak peeks of future books.

Keep reading for an excerpt from Dean Blake Morris's book…

I JOGGED UP the steps of the farm-style house in good spirits. I let myself in using my key and called out, "Mr. Morris! It's Erin."

Call me Blake, he always said, but for some reason I couldn't.

I wasn't usually a stickler for propriety, but with him it seemed like a good idea.

Maybe his military roots made the formality seem right to me.

Or more likely, it was the domesticity of

cleaning his home. The barrier of his last name was little defense against my attraction.

It would be so easy to slip, to let him see how I felt about him. Then I'd feel like an idiot—a hopeless little girl dreaming about a man almost old enough to be my father.

I pulled a book from my bag and went upstairs in search of my boss. The pages were well-worn when he gave it to me. Even more so after I read it. Three times. I could probably put it in his bookcase, always neat and organized, so I'd know right where it belonged. In fact, his entire house sparkled from the knotted floorboards to the arched ceilings.

It was partly because he was neat, but also because I came twice a week. It was one of the odd habits that made my reclusive employer so strange, and also endearing.

He never left a mess, but he didn't want me to come less often.

Not that I could complain. I needed the money.

Well, I could replace the book on my own, but I wouldn't. The truth is that I wanted an excuse to talk to him. We had a lively debate on the merits of the U.N. in my political science class yesterday, and I knew he'd have insights on it.

Blake Morris was a Rhodes scholar and famed military strategist. He was also named as a likely successor to his father's dynasty empire. That was before. Before he was hit with an IED and burned over thirty percent of his body. Since then, he'd lived in seclusion, not teaching, barely ever leaving his house.

Poking my head into his bedroom, I found him there.

In a manner of speaking.

My breath caught as I took in the sight.

He lay spread out on the bed, his skin still drop-dappled from a shower, a white towel fell open around his waist. The tanned skin and flexing muscles. The fist he made.

Oh God.

He was masturbating.

Shit.

This was so wrong.

And strangely beautiful.

He was like some Adonis. Old-world artists would have wanted to create a statue out of marble. I should leave. This was clearly a private moment.

He wouldn't want me to see this. Not only because of his obvious nakedness but because of the scars I could see. They continued down the side of his face, his neck, onto his muscled torso, the outside of his thigh.

I really should turn around, walk away, and absolutely, positively not watch.

Instead, I stood there, my eyes riveted to his exposed cock standing up thick from his fisted hand. "God, baby," he moaned, his eyes closed. "Suck it, please."

My lips parted in surprise as if I could obey him from across the room.

My sex throbbed to hear his rasping voice say those dirty words, to watch his hand fist his cock. It was shocking and invasive and so compelling that I wanted to fall to my knees.

"Yes. Yesss. So beautiful. God." His other hand reached to cup his balls. "That's right, baby. Lick them. Suck them."

My gaze flew to his face, mesmerized by the interplay of shiny, scar tissue and ruddy, healthy skin twisted in a grimace of pleasure. His burns and coarse features might make him intimidating to some people, but when I looked at him, I saw only Blake, with his brilliant ideas and gruff kindness, with his harsh sensuality.

"Touch yourself. Yeah, yeah. Take me deep in your mouth and stick your fingers in your cunt. Make yourself feel good, beautiful."

His eyes were shut, lashes fanning over his masculine cheeks.

Who was he imagining kneeling in front of him?

My thighs squeezed together where I stood, giving myself what relief I could. If I moved, either my legs or my hands, I'd have to acknowledge that what I was doing, that watching was wrong, so I stayed very still.

Then, shockingly, he moaned my name, "Erin…"

I barely had time to process that, and then he came, spurting into his cupped hand.

My whole body clenched hard, not quite an orgasm, more like an echo. The suggestion of climax. An involuntary sound escaped me—a whimper, almost.

Heavy lids slid open as he turned to look at me. His eyes widened into a look of shock, even horror. He looked angry, and of course, of course he should be. He should be furious.

Mortified, I turned and ran down the stairs. The sound of my name hurtled down the steps after me, not in passion this time, but I couldn't go back. I invaded his privacy in the worst way.

Maybe finding him had been an accident.

Staying had been unforgivable.

Even knowing that, I couldn't say I'd act differently.

Part of me wanted to run outside, to climb into my car, and drive away. But I needed this job, if there was any hope of keeping it, I'd have to stay. My scholarship covered tuition, but not the rent on my small apartment, not the electric bill or textbooks or gas to get to school.

And more than that, I needed to apologize to him.

Blake Morris had always been decent to me. Always kind.

He didn't deserve my ogling him.

Pacing in the kitchen, I battled my embarrassment at being caught in a compromising position. Or rather, how I'd caught him in a compromising position. I'd have to face him, but I wouldn't look for him. Not right then and maybe not ever. I'd just have to live here in the kitchen, for ten minutes or ten hours.

For ten years, if that's how long it takes for him to come downstairs.

My hands gripped the stone edge of the countertops, then smoothed across the surface. Already clean, as usual. I'd run my rags over the shiny granite until it gleamed. That's what I should have done instead of looking for him. Why did I even think he'd be interested in hearing about my class? Or my thoughts about the book?

I'd never done anything quite this embarrassing. Watching a man's private moment? That's low. And even worse, I respected him so much.

I liked him, and I might have ruined everything.

Want to read more? Find BEAUTY AND THE PROFESSOR at Amazon, Apple Books, and other bookstores!

Books by Skye Warren

Endgame Trilogy & more books in Tanglewood

The Pawn

The Knight

The Castle

The King

The Queen

Escort

Survival of the Richest

The Evolution of Man

Mating Theory

The Bishop

North Security Trilogy & more North brothers

Overture

Concerto

Sonata

Audition

Diamond in the Rough

Silver Lining

Gold Mine

Finale

Rochester Trilogy & more
Private Property
Strict Confidence
Best Kept Secret
Hiding Places
Behind Closed Doors

Chicago Underground series
Rough
Hard
Fierce
Wild
Dirty
Secret
Sweet
Deep

Stripped series
Tough Love
Love the Way You Lie
Better When It Hurts
Even Better
Pretty When You Cry
Caught for Christmas

Hold You Against Me
To the Ends of the Earth

The Modern Fairy Tale Duet
Beauty and the Professor
Falling for the Beast

**For a complete listing of Skye Warren books,
visit**

www.skyewarren.com/books

About the Author

Skye Warren is the bestselling author of dangerous romance such as the Endgame trilogy. Her books have been on the New York Times, the USA Today, and the Wall Street Journal bestseller lists. They feature powerful men and the strong women who bring them to their knees. She makes her home in Texas with her loving family, sweet dogs, and flying squirrel.

Sign up for Skye's newsletter:
skyewarren.com/newsletter

Like Skye Warren on Facebook:
facebook.com/skyewarren

Join Skye Warren's Dark Room reader group:
skyewarren.com/darkroom

Follow Skye Warren on Instagram:
instagram.com/skyewarrenbooks

Visit Skye's website for her current booklist:
skyewarren.com/books

COPYRIGHT

This is a work of fiction. Any resemblance to actual persons, living or dead, business establishments, events or locales is entirely coincidental. All rights reserved. Except for use in a review, the reproduction or use of this work in any part is forbidden without the express written permission of the author.

The Student © 2024 by Skye Warren
Print Edition

Formatting by BB eBooks
Cover by Book Beautiful
Proofreading by Sisters Get Lit.erary

www.ingramcontent.com/pod-product-compliance
Lightning Source LLC
Chambersburg PA
CBHW050529110726

47899CB00005B/1654

9 781645 961116